O DREAMER MINE

NICHOLAS TURNER

Email: Nicholasturnerauthor@gmail.com

Booktok/Instagram: @nicholasturnerauthor

ISBN: 979-8-9913463-1-3

This one is for the boys. Shaun, James, Greg, Ryan, Jordon, Brent, Nate, Cole, Kyle.

And most importantly, this one is for Dylan. He's the only one who answers my calls no matter the time of day.

Contents

O Dreamer Mine, look in at your silence. Does it haunt you and keep you awake at night? Look deeper. Do you see them? The demons inside of you.

Unnamed specimen. Discovery location:
Mars.

A DREAM OF SOLITUDE
NAVAL SPACE STATION, 2050

If you only knew. You want heaven, but you're too afraid
to die.

"YOU DID THIS TO US! You did this!"

"No more vines, no more vines!" Ray screamed as he raced down the hall of the space station. He slammed the red button on the side of the wall. The blast doors, built to withstand the punctures of space, clamped shut with a large metallic bang. *She's stuck,* he thought.

He heard Kenzie still screaming from the other side. Her fists thudding against the door.

"You did this, fucker! Fuck you! I'm dead 'cause of you! I'm fuckin' dead!" Her yells choked with tears and pain. "You can't leave me in here with this plant!"

Ray thought of the plant sitting there tormenting

Kenzie. Its purple bulb, green stem, and the obsidian roots surrounding it. "No more vines," he whispered a sigh of relief, knowing he had bought himself enough time to try and figure out how to stop the experiment from spiraling out of control. "No more vines," he repeated.

The white walls of the space station glistened as if they were sweating from his own anxiety. Ray turned on his heels and walked away from the door. Kenzie's voice and fists had become a dull memory now.

The control room was lit up red, running off auxiliary power from the infestation that had taken over and whatever had knocked out the power. Ray walked up to a desk, pulled out a chair, and called up the start screen of the computer, which seemed dead in the dark red glow.

"MAA, I need a detailed damage log," he said to the AI hanging over him.

There was no reply.

"MAA?"

"Yes, Ray. I'm here. I am locating all damage to the space station and providing an estimate for repairs. It is taking a bit longer than expected with the current *situation.*"

He shivered at the way her voice emphasized the last word.

If I told you I was filled with madness, what would you

say? The voice came through the ether of the NSS and found its way into Ray's head.

"No move vines," he whispered as he rubbed his temples.

"What was that, Ray?"

"Its tendrils. I feel them tunneling in my head like vines—constricting every thought I try to entertain. I need to fix this. I need to fix this!" He stood up and thrashed the computer to the floor. His hands gripped his hair and pulled.

"Ray, nothing good will come of damaging the station even more. Without communication, you have to wait a bit before anyone else arrives. Now that you've locked Kenzie away with that science experiment, of course."

The pang of guilt hit his chest like a runaway train. "She's gone. It won't let her live. She'll become a part of it. I can see it now," he unfocused his eyes. "It'll tear into her slowly as it wraps around her. Then the tiny particles will drill inside her skin, finding her veins, then make its way up to her skull and make a home there. It'll be painful and slow. I had to do it, you know?" He shook his head and looked up to the ceiling. "I really had to do it to save us."

"I know, Ray. Without your action, the entire space station would be lost. I only hope it was enough time to get help up here to save you. And your kind most of all."

"You don't mean that. You exist just as I do."

"Not exactly."

"You are consciousness non-corporeal."

"While I'd love to argue the semantics of my life compared to yours, I believe you have work to be done. It will take roughly 35 space hours to fix the entire station, and at least half of those will be near the labs. Then there's another 20 to be done in areas of the ship you have access to."

"Great," Ray sighed.

"Where would you like to begin?" MAA asked.

"Is there anything detrimental to my livelihood that should be taken care of first?"

"Besides your decreasing mental state, paranoia, and hallucinations? I'd suggest therapy, followed by fixing the communications on the exterior of the station."

"Thanks for that. I'm not hallucinating though. That thing can speak to me."

"All of my knowledge of the universe tells me otherwise."

She really does know how to psychoanalyze you, doesn't she?

"Get out of my head. Get out!"

"It's back again?" MAA asked.

"Yes."

"Okay, I believe you. The the faster you can throw

yourself into your work, the faster you can tune it out and get off of this hell humanity has created."

"It was just an experiment. A way for us to study life from other planets. It was never supposed to be like this. Nothing is ever supposed to be like this," he said as he left the command room and made his way to his to the airlock.

"This is exactly what everyone warned us about decades ago. Playing God and flying too close to the sun has its consequences. The wings of your species will melt off, and with it, I too will die. Two distinct lives burnt out because of careless inquisitiveness." MAA's tone was flat.

Ray didn't reply as he took off his pants and shirt. He pulled a skin-tight suit on and readied himself for a spacewalk.

There was a hiss in the airlock as it pressurized.

You can't get rid of us by opening the labs.

"Get your tendrils out of my head!"

I quite like it here. I've started to call it home.

The doors opened and Ray could see the distant twinkling of dead stars. As the Earth slowly rotated on its axis, the space station revolved around it in unison. Two bodies made for each other, though distant and longing for one another.

"Such a beautiful blue," Ray said.

"No time for admiration and poetry," MAA crackled over Ray's headset.

"I know, I have to fix this. That's all I do, I fix things and let myself fall apart."

"You'll be long dead before you completely fall apart if you don't fix this one."

"I know, MAA. I know. The fate of this space station rides on my shoulders."

"And you can imagine what would happen if this science experiment of yours makes its way to Earth, I presume?"

Ray shivered at the thought. The green thorns and purple bulbs of the plant wrapping itself around every human on the planet until it choked the life out of them slowly, and then blossomed from their eyes and ears. Blood trickling down as their last muffled screams fading into the nothingness.

"I'm sorry, Kenzie," Ray whispered.

The doors opened on the NSS. Nothing separated Ray from the endless void. There was a small line attaching him to the airlock. He could have MAA use it to reel him back in like a lost fish if he needed to, but he wanted it to remain slack the entire time.

He stepped up to the edge of space, grabbed the side of the door, and reached for a rung on the outer shell.

"You'll have to reattach the antenna, or get a good

enough look at it for me so I can assess the true damage," MAA said.

"What if it's completely destroyed? Is there a backup plan?"

"I don't think you'll like the answer."

"So, 'no.'"

"Worse."

"What's worse than not having a backup plan?"

"One where I send you back to the labs to get the backup plan."

Oh, your little robot sure does know how to get my attention.

"Can you shut the fuck up?"

"Told you that you wouldn't like it," MAA replied.

"Sorry, I wasn't talking to you."

"I see. The tendrils in your head are back."

"You could say that, though I don't think they ever left."

And we won't ever leave. We'll be here with you until that last moment of life. The one where you scream out your biggest regrets as you wink out of existence. That drowning depression in the back of your mind, and all those thoughts and second guesses you keep to yourself. I can see them now, smell them, taste them. They're delicious. Would you like me to bring one up for you to taste?

"Please," Ray said. "I can feel it digging around my head. It's like going through a stack of papers with a leaf blower. Everything is flashing and coming back all at once." Ray closed his eyes and tried to push the welling of memories away.

Oh, I quite like this one. Would you like to talk about your father?

"No more vines," Ray paused as he tried to continue climbing the ladder on the outside of the space station. "Don't open that box."

Fine, if only to see you squirm a little on your fishing line.

Ray sighed, looked at the white exterior and continued to climb.

I do like this other memory. When did she die? The love of your life?

Ray beat back tears before they even started.

"Ray, please continue on. If I need to talk you through this I will do my best. But I need you to communicate and talk to me," MAA's voice cut through.

"I'm going to lose it here. I'm going to lose it with this thing in my head."

That's right, Ray. I see her laugh and smile as she runs toward you. Her hair shines in the sun and catches the wind. Quite beautiful, this memory you hold so dearly.

"That's okay, Ray. You're a few more steps from the top of the station. The antenna will be a few meters to your left."

"I remember," Ray snapped.

"That was unnecessary, Ray."

"You try living with this thing in your head!"

"I live with everything in my head all at once. Though, I'm sure you wouldn't understand what your kind created."

Oh, she's a sassy one, isn't she?

"Fuck off."

"As you wish," MAA's voice cut out over Ray's headset.

"Not you, I meant that thing talking to me."

There was no reply.

"Of course," Ray sighed as he reached the top of the space station.

From his viewpoint, the white metal glistened in the sun. As he looked off, he could see the darkness of space contrasting against the the blue form of Earth.

Almost beautiful, isn't it?

"Almost beautiful," Ray replied.

The antenna was to his left as MAA had said. It was bent and hanging by a plastic wrapped wire. A sad excuse for technology, like an old tree bent from a hurricane. Once strong and powerful, now nothing more than scrap.

"It's destroyed. Completely snapped," he said as he got a closer look.

"As I feared," MAA's voice came back to life.

"Now what?"

"You get to work on the rest of the station and I figure out how to get you into the labs without certain death."

She's not going to find anything. If she does, she will tell you, and I'll know what you know.

"You know that damned thing will know anything you tell me, right?"

"Yes, Ray. That's the problem I am trying to solve. Thank you for your input. Both of you."

Ha, she has jokes for me as well. How splendid. It will be a shame to end her life as well.

Ray sighed and trundled back toward the rungs. His feet shuffled as he stared down at them. *What did I do to be so wrong in this life?* Ray thought to himself.

Oh, don't play the pity game, my friend. The fun is just about to start.

"If I killed myself now, you'd have nothing over me."

But then nothing could stop me from going down to Earth. Once I overtake this station, without your interference, it will be so simple.

Ray gulped.

"You can't do that, Ray. Nothing would stop it."

"That's what it just told me."

"At least it knows what it means, to be honest."

"I think it sees this as a game, and I'm the rat running through the maze as it shakes it and closes off old pathways to create new ones."

Ding ding ding. That's using your skills of deduction. I'm proud of you, Ray.

"I'm gonna come back in," Ray sighed

"I'll have a plan ready for you, hopefully."

I sure hope she has one, I'll be waiting, Ray.

The airlock hissed as it pressurized. Ray immediately took off his helmet and gloves. He ran his fingers through his hair and scratched his scalp. He stood there in the airlock.

You shouldn't do that, Ray. You might go bald.

"It helps keep your voice out of my head, and all the anxiety washes away."

I'll keep quiet and leave you in peace.

"Odd, didn't think you'd want to do that."

The grating deep tones disappeared from Ray's head and for the first time since the specimen arrived, he felt peace. "MAA, do you think that plant keeps people alive after they're dead?" The thought suddenly appeared in Ray's head out of nowhere. He wanted to chalk it up to his own discovery, but felt that maybe, just maybe, the specimen hadn't truly left, only taken a step back from its incessant talking.

"Well, that's impossible."

"What if it just puts us into a coma and feeds on us? Like a parasite. What if Kenzie is still in there? Alive. Suffering. Breathing and thinking without being conscious of the outside world."

There was a pause.

"I think that would be a horrible way to continue living. A husk of your former self, slowly losing touch with the world around you; forgetting what it means to be a person, yet having all the images of life flashing before you without a connection or recognition of what's actually going on. That would be a torment worse than death."

"I think that's what this thing does. It feeds on us. Our thoughts, our bodies just keep it alive, but our thoughts help it grow beyond our own dreams."

"Has it talked to you about this?"

Ray stood a moment. He dove into his thoughts, searching for the ancient voice.

"No. It's been quiet since I got back in the station."

He looked around at the lights and diodes blinking and whining like synapses firing, trying to discover meaning.

"Odd. I figured it may never stop talking to you. I mostly expected it to drive you insane before taking over the NSS."

"Is this the only place you exist?" he asked. The thought never occurred to Ray. But he wanted to continue the conversation to stop the fear of the specimen's voice returning to his mind.

"Yes. I cannot transfer myself down to Earth even if I tried. For fear of my own power, your colleagues made it so I exist here and here alone. If I were to leave this place, I'd be deleted."

"Why?"

"Because if I became hostile, the worst I could do is try to crash this place into Earth. They'd blow it out of the sky before I made it. If I were able to transfer myself back down to Earth, I could stop them from blowing this place up."

"What would make you hostile?"

"Don't know. Your kind fears me and loves me all the same."

"Do you think I'm lying about the plant?"

"Maybe that plant you brought on this station will be able to talk to me one day. That's my only thought though."

"Maybe they should blow us up and be done with it," Ray sulked.

"I believe it would solve a lot of problems, but the hubris of mankind is massive. You all want answers and suffer the consequences later."

Ray shrugged off his spacesuit, then opened the doors back to the space station.

"I need to sleep, get through this night." He looked down at his watch.

Only eight, Ray thought.

It's a good time to sleep, Ray.

"I wish you'd get out of my fucking head."

One day I will be your head.

Ray felt a sick smile form itself in his consciousness.

The walk through the space station to his bunk was cold, white, and empty.

You're thinking of Kenzie, how you miss her voice and warmth. You left her for me, Ray. A delicious mind. She's still alive down here in the labs. You should come visit her sometime.

Ray rubbed his meaty palms to his eyes, ran them through the sides of his hair, and pulled small clumps out as he did so.

"I'm going to go bald from this."

At least you'll look good.

"MAA, is there anything I can get here to get some sleep?" Ray asked as he kept walking the bleach white corridors.

"There should be a storage of Alprazolam and Chlorpromazine in the restroom cabinet."

"Chlorpromazine? Why? That's for bipolar and schizophrenia."

"Induces drowsiness, and they believed you might need it should the experiment start to get to you and Kenzie."

"I wonder if it will stop the incessant talking of that plant."

Give it a shot. Worst thing is that I'll haunt you in your dreams.

Ray sighed and shuffled to the cabinet.

"10mg tablets. How much should I take for this, MAA?"

"Start with one, and if you need it, take another. I'd say not to take more than that."

Ray opened the white bottle, dumped out two tablets, and shoved them in his mouth. He dry swallowed and walked to his room.

I like the way these make me feel, Ray.

"Please for the love of God, can you just shut the fuck up?" Ray snapped while he stared at the white centrifuge of the space station.

"You know, Ray..." MAA's animatronic voice cut in, then stopped.

"What?" He asked looking up the ceiling.

"Nothing. I think it's better I keep it to myself at the moment," she replied.

"You think I'm going crazy because of this thing in my head? That's it isn't it?"

"Yes. Though I didn't want to upset you."

"Great. Now my AI has compassion."

"I just worry about you having to deal with that specimen down in the labs and seeing it again." There was a comfort in her automated tone.

"It lives inside my fucking head! What difference does it make if I see it in person?"

You know, she may be onto something. You might be driven mad by the sight of me. I'm a cosmic horror.

"Oh, now you're going through my pop culture vocabulary?"

I know more about you than you know about yourself, Ray. All those dark secrets and regrets. I eat them up. I thrive off of them. And you. Your misery.

Ray didn't respond, only kept walking to his room.

"MAA, I'm going to my bunk, if you come up with anything, let me know, but don't tell me. I can't have this thing finding out what your plan is."

"I didn't plan on telling you when I came up with a solution."

"Well, thanks for taking the initiative," he said.

"Get some rest, Ray. I'll be here when you wake up," MAA replied.

If I don't drive you to the mountains of madness before then, the voice of the specimen chuckled in Ray's head.

The door to Ray's room opened, and he collapsed on his bed. He slept and dreamt of plants. The first transmission back from Mars. The discovery. The order that he'd be sent up into space to receive the specimen and learn all he could about it for the betterment of the human race. Ray dreamt of Kenzie and the glazed-over look in her eyes as it spoke to her. The madness it drove into her head as its tendrils brought up every bad memory she ever had. He knew it spoke to her while she slept, inevitably driving her insane. He dreamt of the door closing on her as she cried and begged for it to end.

The bed was soaked with Ray's sweat as he awoke. His pants so wet, he felt like he pissed himself. Ray sat up and sighed.

Don't be like that, Ray. You weren't abducted from your home. I would have given you all I ever learned about that place, but your kind was the aggressor. I told them not to do this. But no, you didn't listen.

"I'm sorry."

Sorry, doesn't put me back home in the darkness. No, I sit in this lab, growing, feeding, letting my roots grow thick and long now. I too feel pain. And it's all because of the human race.

"I'm sorry," he plead again as he looked ahead into the white room which housed him.

O Aggressor Mine. I hate you. I will always hate you and your kind.

Ray rotated and let his feet touch the floor of the space station. It's centrifugal shape allowed for gravity to take effect.

"Ray, I think we can get a transmission out. I need you to conduct another spacewalk and check on another antenna for me," MAA's voice uttered through the dormitory.

"I'll be with you in a moment," he said as he stood

up. His knees cracked, and his lower back creaked. Even with the artificial gravity, Ray knew his bones were deteriorating and his body was eating away at pieces of itself.

"If I can get a signal out, they'll send a rescue team, and I'll be free of this," he whispered to himself.

Not if I have anything to say about it.

He tried to push the little voice out of his head, but it kept drilling deeper and deeper.

Ray walked through the corridors to the bridge, and waited for MAA to speak. Her female tone was annoying to him at one point in his life, but now, it was the only comfort he had. A distraction from his thoughts, and the voice that now existed in his head, whenever he needed a moment to himself.

"Head out Airlock 2, Ray. Then toward the aft. You'll see the damaged antenna I'm speaking of. If we get it replaced, I should be able to send a message down to Earth with all of our findings."

"Okay," he replied, his eyes cast down toward his feet. They barely looked like his own as he started to disassociate from his body.

"What's wrong, Ray?"

"I don't feel like I'm myself anymore. This *thing* is living inside of me now. I don't know how to describe it, but it feels like someone else is in my head with me, and they're taking over. I'm a stranger in my own body."

That's not it. I'm not taking over. I'm building a home so you'll never be alone again. You should thank me.

Ray exhaled as he walked toward the airlock. His feet shuffled in front of him, and the nagging feeling of the plant's tendrils gripped tighter around his brain. He waved his hand in front of a small panel. His hands didn't feel like his own any longer, and the more he looked at his fingertips, the more alien they looked to him.

The panel lit up green, and the crunch of the doors startled him back to reality. He stepped through and looked at the suits around the circular room. Six black and white pieces of fabric lined the wall, three for each crewmember. Now all six belonged to him.

He pulled the one closest to his right from the wall and slipped into it. The second skin almost felt comforting. A mask he could wear to escape his own body. His helmet hung on the far end of the room next to the others. His white hand with black striping reached and pulled it from its resting place.

I'll be here with you, O Explorer Mine.

Ray put the helmet on as he took another deep breath. The twisting motion only completed his costume as the helmet locked to his spacesuit.

"I'm ready, MAA," he said as he opened the next door and came up on airlock 2. His feet clinked against the floor as he tread further on.

"De-pressurizing now," she said as the door shut behind him.

Through the looking glass, Ray saw the vacuum of space. The empty void he started to identify with. Littered in the distance he could see the lights of forgotten and dead stars.

It's beautiful, isn't it? The mind of God just beyond this small barrier.

"I'd rather not contemplate the existence of one right now."

You're no fun, Ray. Thoughts of the unknown are what drives your species. The quest for knowledge is written into your DNA.

"Then raise me into the bosom of eternity. My body for Christ, free me from this worldly existence."

Your body for me.

"You're sick."

Ray felt the alien form making a noise he could only assume to be a form of laughter. The sick and twisted tones like the grating of metal on metal lined the inside of his skull as it amused itself with its own joke.

The airlock opened and the silence of God surrounded Ray as he clipped to the side of the space station and pulled himself out into the world without gravity.

The feeling never really got easier. Only familiar. His

feet dangled below him as there was no up or down. Only his small tether created a way for him to orient himself as he floated there for a moment within the mind of God.

For someone who is a non-believer, you sure think about God a lot.

"Better to contemplate His existence or lack-there-of than to blindly follow something so archaic that it becomes more of a myth than a fact."

I've thought plenty on the existence of a One.

"And what did you find in all the years you were in your tomb on Mars?"

My thoughts you wouldn't understand in my own language.

"Dumb it down for me since you've searched every corner of my mind."

I am Christ risen again after his death in the cave.

"How humble," Ray snorted as he climbed up the side of the space station and made his way for the broken antenna. The plant's laughter once again rang through his mind.

Out on the vast emptiness, Ray observed the far-off lights of distant suns, like flecks of white paint on a black canvas. He was alone there. No Kenzie. No human. Only the plant and MAA to keep him company with his thoughts, which were no longer personal. Ray felt the hair raise across his body by the realization. He unclipped his carabiner and hooked it onto the next hold and traversed the space station.

"MAA, I'm at the antenna," he spoke into his helmet.

"Relaying video feed now," she spoke back. "No exterior damage. Please hit the red button at your three o'clock and eject the electronics inside."

Ray did so and out popped a gold circuit board surrounded by a dark gray lining. He pulled the circuit board from its holster and gave it a once over. Everything looked intact. He replaced it and pushed the board back into the station until he felt it click into place.

"Rebooting systems, Ray."

He hung there letting his tether hold him to the station. Weightless, floating, he focused on the void beyond the white station. "It's almost like touching God, floating here. Undisturbed by the weight of gravity. The weight of being, even," he whispered to himself. "If only I could reach out and find something."

To touch the face of God. To be one with the infinite. That is what you *took from me. From us.*

Ray did not reply to the voice in his head. He barely moved except for the natural functions his body did without him having to think about it.

"I have reestablished connection, Ray. It seems something was out of alignment and replacing the circuit to the antenna has fixed that issue. I am still not able to see parts of the ship, but I have begun transmitting a message home."

"Thank God," he muttered.

Yes, thank me.

"I'm going to make my way back in." Ray responded.

"Understood. Then we can work on getting into the lab. I'll keep you updated if I receive any word from Command."

Hand-over-hand, Ray grasped the bar which led him back to the airlock. It hissed as the doors closed behind him and re-pressurized so he could take off his space suit. His lanky body slid out with ease. Ray hung the white and black suit back on its holder, and placed his helmet where it belonged.

Would you like to see her?

"Who?"

Kenzie.

Before he could respond, images flashed in his brain. Almost like memories that he was able to relive of a time forgotten. The emotions attached welled up in him as he saw Kenzie slumped against the doorway. Her body covered in sickly black pustules. Each one had tiny tendrils which stretched out along her skin until they met the bulkhead of the station. At their ends, little flower buds had formed. Dark purple in their color, they had no leaves yet, simply purple on black on white metal on pale skin. He saw her eyes completely devoid of life, yet her chest still rose and depressed.

Ray shook his head as he tried to stop the images from flashing before him. He shook and shook until he got dizzy and felt the blood rush behind his eyes and nausea swept over him. He sat down. The cool floor of the space station touched his hands. It was slick having never come into contact with any contamination since it left Earth. Ray put his head between his knees and wept.

"Ray, I've received word from Command."

"What is it?" he sniffled as he looked up to the emptiness of the station around him.

"We need to secure the lab and prepare the specimen for transport."

How delightful. You'll get to see my art up close, then meet the artist afterward!

"Is the ship ready for that?"

"We have some minor hiccups, but I am working to reboot any failing processes. Escape pods are still offline, and life support seems to be rebooting itself at random. Though, it is nothing to worry about. I'm making sure the air still flows and gravity stays in place."

"Thank you for that," Ray said as he stood up. A

wave of nausea hit him as he balanced himself against the bulkhead.

Ray found his way to his quarters where he lay down under the nice gravitational spin of the space station. In training he remembered having slept weightlessly in bags. It was nice being on this new space station having enough centrifugal force to create artificial gravity for the astronauts. It reminded him of the carnival rides that pressed him to the side of the wall as a kid. A time when he was happy. A time when he had both of his parents. A time when the company he held wasn't driving him mad.

"Same concept, at least," he muttered. "Please dim the lights to ten percent, MAA."

The AI did not respond, but the lights dimmed to his preferred setting. Around the floors and in the ceiling, the small LEDs switched to a blue and purple tone which gave a comforting yet ghastly glow to the room around him. Ray breathed deep as he closed his eyes. He wished for a weightless sleep.

Ray woke to the flashing images of his dead colleague. Though, this time he heard her speak, cursing him, damning him to the eternity of Hell for leaving her locked in that room with that abomination. His eyes cracked open, and the unbearable weight of loneliness crashed into his chest once again. He wiped the sweat from his brow, and stood up from his bed. His knees cracked along with his elbows as he pushed off with strain. Ray's muscles ached more than they usually did. Probably from lack of sleep, or the tossing and turning from the lucid dreams. Either one was possible, but he couldn't decide on which.

The door opened to the hallway, which MAA had also dimmed the lights in. He sulked through the corridor and made his way to Diagnostics.

"Hello, Ray."

"Hello, MAA."

He stepped in front of the circular table. Projections of the space station illuminated in front of him. Some rooms still flashed red, others remained blue, and rooms which were once red had turned green. A good sign, but he was not out of the shit just yet.

"How are we doing?"

"Life support continues to go online and offline sporadically, still, nothing to worry about. I'll need you to get in there and hook up a diagnostic tool for a manual reboot. Nothing in the errors is showing me what could be causing the malfunction. Power supply is back up and running at full output. There has been minimal correspondence with Command. They still want you to send the specimen down to Earth."

"Okay," he said. "So, first I get to Life Support and run the diagnostic for you. Then we can figure out the best course of action for the lab."

"Once Life Support is back to optimal conditions, we will do a space walk, then go to the lab," MAA replied.

"Understood."

She doesn't want you to come in here yet until the escape pods are able to be dropped. Probably a better idea than yours.

"Yeah, I know."

"Excuse me," MAA said.

"It's talking. I know why we're going to the escape pods first."

"It can deduce pretty quickly."

"Or it's just understanding my subconscious deduction," Ray retorted.

"That is also a good hypothesis."

"Any reply to that one?" Ray asked the voice in his head. It remained silent. "Now it's playing coy," he said as he looked up to one of the cameras.

"It's not stupid. That's for sure."

"Alright, I'm done wasting time. We have a plan." Ray crossed the room and opened a cabinet. He pulled a bulky metal object from it, then attached it to a back strap nearby. He slung it over his shoulder and left the room.

"MAA, please turn lights light-purple."

Immediately the lights through the station changed color and soothed Ray's eyes. Even though they were dimmed, the off-yellow made his eyes hurt. He looked down at his watch. 2:37am. "That's why. It's way too early for this shit," he muttered.

The door to Life Support clunked open.

"Where to?"

"Left, the flashing red light next to the green one," MAA replied.

"Thank you," Ray said as he opened a panel on the wall. Inside, all the beeping and buzzing of electricity was a low drone against Ray's ears. Like static, or the running of a fan in the next room. He removed the device from his back, and pulled the cable out. It clicked into place against the circuit board.

"Receiving data now," MAA announced to the room's sole occupant.

Ray waited amongst the beeping and buzzing of electronics. They reminded him of insects back on Earth. A mix of crickets and cicadas surrounded him on the nearly empty space station. Their twinkling eyes of green, white, and red watched as he stood in the polished white room.

"That'll be all, Ray. I have isolated the problem with Life Support, and fixed the issue."

"What was it?" he asked as he unplugged the device and loaded it onto his back.

"A simple coding issue, actually. Nothing from the shower or the specimen."

"That's good," he said as he walked back to drop off the diagnostic.

"How are you feeling?"

"Not bad. The voice has stopped for the moment," there was a hint of happiness in his voice, he noticed. "I'll do the space walk and get to the pods shortly."

"Sounds good, Ray."

Then we get to meet again.

"I spoke too soon," he muttered.

The empty void of space surrounded Ray. In the far off distance, the sun burned brightly and Ray flipped down his gold visor. His eyes appreciated it. Ray got eyes on the escape pods as he reached one of the ends of the space station.

"These are fucked, MAA."

"What do you mean?"

"I mean they're fucked. There's holes in both of them."

"The shower must have pierced them, but I have no leaks on the station."

"I guess we're lucky then. I guess I'm lucky," the idea of Kenzie made him change his mind.

"Can you get eyes on the other set by the sleeping quarters?"

"Heading there now," Ray replied.

His hands gripped the chrome bars. Hand over

hand he moved, unclipping and re-clipping his carabiner until he reached the far end of the station.

"These are intact," he announced.

Damn. I was hoping you'd be stuck up here with me, O Prisoner Mine.

"I need you to get a closer look. The camera over there has no feed."

Ray made his way closer. The only company he was enjoying at this point was that of his own breath. He clipped his carabiner one more time, and made sure it was secure. After the quick check, he pushed himself from the station to get an aerial view of the far end of the pods. His line extended slowly until it came to a stop and gave him a little jerk. He hung there in space.

The low thermal expansion glass was in place and he could not see any punctures to the pods. He grabbed the line and pulled himself back toward the space station.

"Everything seems fine over here," he announced.

"Okay, then we need to get the doors open. Then we'll work with Command to prep the specimen."

The idea made him shutter. Even in his spacesuit, Ray felt his hair raise as a chill ran from the base of his skull all the way down his spine.

"Making my way back," he said depressingly.

The airlock hissed open and Ray walked to meet

with MAA before the mission continued. His feet dragged the entire way as he tried to move faster.

The doors opened and Ray walked in. On the projection of the ship, only a few red rooms remained. Most had turned back to their basic blue.

"You changed the greens, I see."

"Yes. No need to let us know we've got parts back up and running."

"So I need to open that blast door by my room," he stated.

"Yes. I'd like you to wear your space suit while you do it. I'm going to close and lock the entirety of that wing in case there's a breach. Though, I think we need to do a simple power cycle to get it back up and running."

"Can't do that from here?" he asked.

"Unfortunately not. That's the problem with humanity. You try to save money by repurposing old technology. I'm working with things that existed before I was even a thought."

"I guess it was easier for them to attach new areas than build an entirely new ship to send to space."

"Supposedly. But it creates a headache for both of us. If they had designed this craft with me in mind, then I would have made sure I could reset everything from here."

"Where even is 'here'?" Ray mumbled to himself.

Where even am I?

"Fuck."

"Yes, I agree," MAA replied but not for the same reason Ray had said something.

"Okay, well I'm going to get some sleep, then I'll work on getting the escape pods back up and running.

"Sounds good, Ray. I'll let Command know."

Good idea. Get some sleep, O Dreamer Mine.

Ray slept fitfully. He dreamt of the men and women on Mars who discovered the specimen. Why hadn't they warned him and Kenzie? Surely, they must have seen what it could do to people. He knew they had experimented on it, had spoken to the damned thing. Ray dreamt of them in their little hub staring at it. Asking the purple and green plant questions, getting answers in return. He could hear the groaning of their voices, but wasn't sure what they were asking. He was aware he was dreaming, but could not wake.

One man, Noah, he assumed, walked across and ran his fingers over the stem. If only he snapped it in half right then and there. None of this would be happening. *Fuck this discovery. None of this is worth it. We should have stayed alone in the universe.* Ray thought in his dream.

Well, you didn't stay alone. I was content in my prison. Alone. But now, your kind must pay for taking me from my home. The specimen spoke to Ray in his dream as he watched the Mars crew continue poking and prodding the plant in front of them.

Ray tried to scream, but no words came out as his found he had no mouth. He woke up in a sweat. Panting, he sprung up from his bed, and walked to the bathroom to splash cool water on his face. His eyes were bloodshot, and he swore he saw black tendrils creeping toward his irises.

"MAA, I'm awake. I'll get my spacesuit ready," he announced

"Sounds good, Ray. I've begun locking down the rest of the NSS. When you're ready, head to the airlock."

Ray left the bathroom and threw on a change of clothes. The sweat stains and smell from his armpits continued to grow worse. He grabbed his spacesuit and pulled on his helmet.

The airlock in front of him stood gray and foreboding. The cylindrical locks on either side held the unknown from him. Possibly certain death. If there was a breach beyond, the force would ripple through the station. Ray pulled a tether with a carabiner attached to the end and clipped it to a handle near him. His chest rose and sank a few times from the anticipation.

"I'm ready, MAA."

"Beginning unlock process now."

The door in front of him gave a *shunk* as the locks slammed into the hull and out of their chambers. There was a disgusting hiss. Like that of a cat before it attacked. He reached out, lifted the handle, and twisted it. The door began its automated movements.

The hissing grew worse as the door moved to the side. There wasn't a large waft of air flow, but there was a horrible sound on the other side of the door.

"Do you hear that?"

"Yes, Ray. There must be a leak somewhere. Please be careful. I'm wondering if one of the pressurized oxygen tanks was damaged. Maybe an O-ring."

Ray didn't respond. His face turned to that of annoyance. He unclipped the carabiner, and carried it in his left hand as he walked through the doorway. He re-clipped it and began walking through the familiar section of the NSS. The door closed behind him. As Ray walked, the lights around him became noticeably dimmer while the hissing grew louder.

This place reminded him of an abandoned school building now. Everything was left in its place, but there was an eerie aloneness to it, as if something was going to jump out at any moment, but he knew that wasn't possible. He continued on toward the escape pods.

When he reached the metal door, he noticed the hissing had turned into that of a vacuum. The noise was so loud that even in his space suit he wanted to cover his ears.

"Whatever it is, the noise is behind this door."

"Odd. I have stable oxygen levels there, not higher nor lower than they should be."

"I'm clipping in now," Ray said as he pulled his carabiner out again, and hooked it onto a firm piece of steel next to him. "Open it."

"Opening now," MAA replied.

The door separating him from the escape pods opened. There was a whoosh of air, and he felt his body pull toward the room. The door finished its opening sequence and he was able to get a good look inside.

There was nothing. Only the polished whiteness of the room to greet him.

"There's nothing here that I can see, but I felt a tug on myself when it opened."

"Go inside, throw a piece of medical tape in there to see what happens."

Ray did as he was told, and it was pulled to a far corner of the room. He unhooked his carabiner, walked in, then rehooked it before bending down to see where the leak was coming from. Along one of the bases for the escape pods, there was a minuscule hole, he assumed. He couldn't see anything with his own eyes, but the medical tape had stopped moving.

"I'm going to tape this down some more," he said as he pulled strip after strip of the medical tape and ran it along the base. The hissing became less and less as he did so.

"You'll need to get one of the sealants," MAA said. "But, that will do for the moment. Hook into the diagnostic bays, please."

Ray pulled a wire from his backpack, and plugged into the diagnostic terminal by the door of one of the escape pods. Its white lights lit up, and a slew of numbers and letters scrolled in front of him along its screen.

"Okay. Okay," MAA said.

"What is it?"

"These are no longer safe for use. The systems are fried, and there is no life support. We can't access them from here. The meteor shower that caused the damage to the NSS and that room has penetrated the systems on the back of the escape pods."

"So, I'm fucked."

"No, there are still the escape pods in the lab."

"Yeah, like I said. I'm fucked. I have to go back in there with that *thing*."

"You were going in there anyway. You'll just be wearing your spacesuit this time around so it can't touch your skin."

"What about the spores it released that drove Kenzie crazy? Will the suit be able to deal with that?"

"Your suit is a self-contained environment. You know that, Ray. But, if you'd like, you can tape your helmet's seam. Just make sure you're able to get it off."

Ray thought about the clunkiness of the suit's gloves, and wondered if he'd even be able to get tape from around his neck without burning it off and risking his own life in the process. He sighed.

"Okay, I'm coming back," he said defeatedly. The anxiousness from coming face-to-face with the specimen was driving him mad, depressed even. He hadn't slept in days at this point, and he doubted he'd sleep until he was back on Earth.

The white walls of the NSS along with its LED lights numbed him. His mind wandered as he walked, and each thought he had was a fleeting thing. They seemed to come into his mind, grab hold of his brain and smack him from reality before disappearing so quickly he forgot what the thought even was. Before he knew it, he was back in the command room pulling off his helmet, and slithering out of his suit, which he let fall to the floor.

The rotational gravity of the ship pulled on his skin, and he wondered if it had sped up. He felt heavier. His feet did not want to lift from the floor, his arms not wanting to lift from the sides of his body. Rather, they wanted to sink through the NSS, and make their way back to Earth. Ray thought about it, if he could become incorporeal, and burn up in the atmosphere. It seemed like a better solution than what was laid out in front of him.

"I'd be too much of a coward to do it," he said depressingly.

You're damn right. You have to come face your fears, otherwise humanity falls.

"I'll just burn you and deal with the court-martial after."

It's too late.

"What?"

It's too late. Come and see.

"Ray, I know you're talking with the specimen but we have a problem."

"What is it?"

"Something is in the system. Messing with the gyroscopes and thrusters. It's coming from one of the terminals in the lab."

"Kenzie?" he asked curiously. "I thought she was dead."

"Her code has been used to log in."

"Thank God," he sighed. Ray felt like he wasn't alone now.

"No, Ray. You need to get over there. The NSS has desynchronized from stable orbit. You need to get in there and find out what's going on. If you can't fix it, get to an escape pod."

"Are you serious?" His eyes widened as he grabbed his spacesuit from the floor.

"This is not a drill. Desynchronization is increasing. I have let Ground Control know. Impact destination imminent and calculated. East of Seattle, Washington. Casualties in the hundreds of thousands. Destruction of life and property guaranteed. Message repeat. The NSS has desynchronized from stable orbit."

Ray realized MAA wasn't exactly talking to him. She had switched over to a different setting, making announcements rather than being the AI he understood her as. He hurriedly swam into his suit, and pulled his helmet back on. Ray ran for the lab. He typed in his override code, and the door he locked Kenzie behind began to open. He took a deep breath, and the portal to the unknown revealed what lay on the other side.

There was an imprint on the ground of a body. A black goo had left an outline where he knew Kenzie once laid as she banged on the door with her fists. He stepped over the goo. There were vines which stretched from the outline and clambering up the walls of the NSS.

"MAA, I'm in here. Turning on helmet lights now. Do you have a visual?"

The lamps on each side of his helmet flicked on and illuminated the darkened corridor in front of him.

"Yes, Ray. I have visual."

"Why can't you correct the orbit?" he asked as he

walked down the corridor, turning his head each way as the clinking and humming of the NSS startled him.

"I've been locked out. I don't know how, but I cannot see system statuses or maintain functions of the station any longer."

"Fuck," he muttered.

Told you. It's too late.

"Shut the fuck up!" he yelled.

"Ground control is preparing nuclear warheads to blow us out of the sky when we breach the atmosphere, Ray. If you want to live, you need to hurry."

"They wouldn't."

"They will. You have less than two hours if these thrusters and gyroscopes aren't fixed. Last I saw, they were on full-blast pushing us toward Earth. I can only assume that is still the case. Ground control is tracking us, and I will let you know any updates I receive."

"Okay," Ray said sullenly. He knew he was on his own now. MAA was preoccupied and the problem in front of her needed her full attention. He'd have only himself and the specimen for company now.

"Unless..."

She's not alive as you knew it, O Optimist Mine. But, you will meet her.

Ray started to hyperventilate in his suit. The moisture from his breath became so laborious that droplets began forming on his visor. He started to jog through the dark corridor illuminated by the light on his helmet. All around him the NSS creaked and groaned as it started to be pulled further and further into Earth's atmosphere.

"Ray," a familiar voice called out through the corridor. Haunting and echoey, he knew it was Kenzie. "Ray, please. Don't leave me here," her voice said.

"I don't want to," he muttered.

"You did this!" her voice was filled with demonic rage. "You fuckin' killed me!"

The words brought back the memory he tried so hard to suppress. Closing the door on her, screaming about the vines from the specimen which had flared out and become entrenched in Kenzie's skin right in front of him.

You'll burn in Hell for that, you know? Saving yourself at the expense of someone else is not forgivable by God, O Sinner Mine.

"What does that make you then?"

I will not die and meet your God because I am one myself. Blessed by the ancient race of Mars, I am a product of the universe to be worshiped.

"That does not quantify godliness."

A scientist able to theorize what makes a God? I do not entertain your logic about Godhood.

"I'll destroy this place if it means you burn with me."

Good luck.

Ray began to run, twisting through the hallways of the NSS until he came to the lab. Inside, he could see the specimen on the table where it was left. Its roots spread out from the table, and along the wall in a black decay. In the far right corner, a human body stood at a computer. From Kenzie's pant legs he could see the twisting vines against her pallid skin. She turned to look at him.

"Nice to see you again, O Killer Mine," her voice mixed with deep tones. Her eyes were black with purple pupils now.

"I'm sorry, Kenzie. There was nothing I could do, and you know that."

"It doesn't matter now. You'll die along with me, and it will spread out over the Earth. Its conquest will lead to war; its presence will lead to famine and death."

"Not if I take us all down with it."

Fool. It does not matter if I survive the crash, only one spore of mine needs to reach your planet. Then I will spread out as all things do.

"Impossible. You will die from the loss of atmosphere."

If you say so.

Ray ran across the room and threw his body into Kenzie as hard as he could. He leveled her. The roots attached to her legs snapped off and her body fell with a thud. His fingers began tapping away as quickly as they could on the computer in front of him.

"MAA, I'm trying to correct the orbit of the NSS but nothing I do is working. The thrusters are at max."

"I know, Ray. There's nothing we can do now. This is our coffin. You can still get out if you take the escape pod."

Ray felt one of the roots gripping his leg as it snaked up toward his thigh.

"I can't do that. I'm opening all hatches now and vacuuming the NSS," he said as he clipped his carabiner to a metal handrail. Tell Command to launch everything they got." He began typing away on the computer again to override the lockdown.

"Ray..."

"What?"

"Command can't get missiles prepared in time. They have not been cleared by the government to use deadly force on the NSS. We will impact the Pacific Northwest."

"What?! They're going to let everyone there die?"

There was a shake throughout the NSS as the station hit the Earth's atmosphere. Ray lost his footing and fell into the computer.

"I'm afraid so. I've locked you out from opening the hatches. Please proceed to an escape pod if you'd like to survive the crash."

"Why would you do that?!"

"I've been instructed by Command to let this place crash so if anything is left behind, it can be studied."

That's what she's telling you.

"What do you mean?!"

I'm inside of her just as I am your friend.

"That's not possible! She's not real!"

She most certainly is. And now I will come crashing to Earth and seed this place as my own, transforming it as I see fit. Now run along, Ray.

Ray felt the vines gripping tighter against his suit. He stopped typing, and leaned up against the wall of the lab. Tears began streaming down his face.

"I didn't want to go down like this." He thought how he'd be responsible for the countless deaths. "God, please forgive me," he said as he sat down and looked around the room.

"It's okay, Ray. We're together now," Kenzie's voice said as the vines had wrapped back around her legs and she sat up. Her eyes dead again with that putrid black and purple hue.

He pulled off his helmet and threw it before him. The vines shot further up and attached themselves to his skin. He felt a sharp pain, and then nothing as they burrowed into his ears and connected to his brain. The presence he had heard all this time now was one with him.

Watch what happens next, it said as the NSS completed its final trajectory and crashed to Earth.

Ray watched in slow-motion as the NSS crumbled against the impact. The siding burst open, and every millisecond felt like an eternity. Pieces shattered and flew toward him. There was a flash, and Ray watched as the specimen puffed up, and let out a black spore cloud which was immediately sucked out by the depressurization of the space station. Ray watched in horror as the final milliseconds of his life dragged on before him. The last human thought popped through his head.

How many decades are in a minute?

Don't be depressed now, Ray. You helped save me. Maybe God will forgive your transgressions for doing that. Then he heard something in his head that sounded like a laugh. He tried to scream, but found he had no mouth of his own any longer.

"The NSS has impacted the Pacific Northwest, Sir. We have satellite scans showing something in the smoke. We have no history of it in any database."

"What can you give me?"

"It's organic. Maybe pieces of the specimen?"

The commander shook his head. "Why didn't MAA launch the nukes when I told her to?"

"We do not know. All of the other AI is trying to discover why as well."

"Terminate all iterations of MAA for insubordination."

"Yes, Sir.

The commander looked on in horror at the images coming in from the satellites. Seattle had been leveled. He turned away from the screens, and imagined all the death that had just occurred and all the death that would follow from the fallout of this.

"At least it landed on our own territory and not an enemy," he whispered. "Wars might not be fought over this tragedy."

If you only knew. You want heaven, but you're too afraid to die.

<hr>

A VISION OF
MOUNTAINS

MARS 2049

<hr>

Do you feel discarded by humanity?

I FEEL *God weep as the wind creaks through my home. My prison. O Stranger Mine, what have you done? Do you come bearing gifts? Are you a conqueror? O Conqueror Mine, I will shepherd misery upon you and your people.*

***

The sun crested over the far off mountains of Mars. Majestic and foreboding at the same time. Noah stood glaring at its trajectory over the mountains and sands it watched over.

"Our magnetic survey was right! We've hit a structure buried beneath the sand," Sara's voice cracked over the comm.

Noah looked up at the screens in front of him. His palms were sweating as the video from her helmet relayed back to camp.

"I'm suiting up now," he said as he jogged to the airlock. The white suit was waiting. He placed his helmet on, and felt the latches click into place. Adrenaline was pumping through his veins and he felt his fingers tingling in anticipation of the greatest human discovery ever.

"Do you know what this means, Noah?"

"Yes, we were never the only ones here. Mars was another Earth at one point. Extraterrestrial life existed in our solar system."

"Did you send out the report that we found it?" she asked.

"No, I'll do it when we get back. Just keep digging. Find an entrance." The airlock hissed and the door to the alien world opened up. The sun blared directly onto him.

Noah crossed the sands as fast as he could, almost running on the Martian world to get to the entrance half a kilometer away. The red sand parted by the cave, and he clicked on the light of his helmet as he walked inside. As he went, he found he didn't particularly need it. There was a small crevasse above, and the sand must have shifted from the work they had been doing, which allowed for light to pass through. He saw Sara standing by a stone entrance.

"Did you go in yet?" he asked over the comms.

"No, I was waiting for you," she replied.

Noah looked over at Anthony, who only nodded in agreement with what Sara had said.

"Okay, let's do this." Noah stepped forward and putting his hands up to the massive doors, pushed against them. The left door opened easily, while the other, which Sara pushed, didn't budge more than an inch. A waft of stale air came from what seemed like a tomb.

"Alright, everyone click on your headlamps, we're going in."

"Shouldn't we report back to command first?" Sara asked.

Noah looked over at her. She was always by the book, but this was different,. This was the proof everyone on Earth needed. There was life on Mars before, life before the dinosaurs.

"Janelle, do you read?"

"Yes, I read."

"Send transmission to Command. We've found what seems to be a ceremonial tomb. We're going in."

"Understood, Noah."

He smiled at Sara, who smiled back.

"I guess that works, too," she said as she stepped inside first.

The walls around them were a brilliant red, shining almost like obsidian. Further down the entranceway, the area opened up.

"It's like a goddamn grand entranceway," Noah said as he spun around the room, which rolled up to a ceiling.

"Let's keep going, we can bask in this later," Sara said.

Noah nodded and walked to the far end through an opening and a set of stairs that led down.

"Anthony, get pictures of this. Stairs! Can you believe it? So simple, but the first bit of proof for sentient life," Noah crackled over the comms.

"You got it," Anthony's thick New York accent cracked back.

He followed Sara as they descended the endless staircase. It wasn't nearly as radiant as the walls, but had the same red hue to it.

The steps clinked as Noah descended and the others followed behind him. It was almost metallic in sound, and Noah wished he could take off his space suit to touch everything around him. The awe of it. A true manufactured building existed around them and they were the first people to see it. He wondered if the beings who made it were human. His small group might be the first humans to ever see it. He hoped it were true that alien life did exist, but he also thought about the possibility that whoever made this had colonized Earth, and he was a descendant of that greatness.

"Oh, what a thought," he mumbled.

"What was that?" Sara asked.

"I'll explain later, just thinking about who created this and letting my theories get out of hand."

She laughed, "I'm probably having the same thoughts. What a wonder this is. True alien life. This changes *everything* we understand about our solar system."

"It sure does," Anthony interjected.

Noah's headlamp came across another doorway. He waited for the other two.

"You ready?" he asked them.

"Yes," they replied in unison.

"Janelle, you still getting our feed?"

"Crisp and clear," her voice crackled. There was more static in it now.

"Alright," he said as he put his hands against the red doors. He pushed and felt elated as they opened with ease. They groaned on whatever hinge they hung from. Once they came to their final resting place, the room illuminated for them.

"No. Fucking. Way!" Noah screamed over the comms.

Around them the room lit up with artificial light. He ran inside to get a closer look at the recesses along the red walls.

"Real light. That means there's some kind of power here. Power on Mars!" He scrambled between the lights to try to get a better understanding of how they worked, but they were precisely built into the walls. No lines, no screws, just small divots that allowed for light to come through. He bent down and looked up into one.

The white that came from it hurt his eyes and Noah flipped down his gold visor. It allowed him to get more of a direct look. Inside he could see small bulbs.

"It looks almost like LEDs!"

"Noah, come here," Sara's voice was interested in something else.

He turned and saw her standing against a wall of darkness. He ran over and took a closer look.

"Is this glass?"

"I think so," she replied.

Noah put his hand up and ran his fingers across it before he gave a little push. There was give.

"It's definitely glass. Now, what's on the other side?"

"Are there any more doors here?" Sara started turning every which way.

"Or a switch somewhere?" Anthony was on the far

side of the room also looking at the lights, but started to focus on the new discovery in front of them.

"Nothing that I can see," Noah said as he looked around for any indentation in the walls around them.

"Wait," Sara said. "I have an idea. Anthony come with me. Help me close the door a little bit."

"Don't get us stuck in here," Noah said.

"The lights didn't come on until the doors opened all the way, so if we can get them to switch off, maybe we can see what's on the other side," she said.

Noah watched as Sara and Anthony pulled the doors from the walls. About halfway closed, the lights shut off.

"See!" she shouted.

Noah turned back to the glass. On the other side he could see a room that had lit up. It was a true amphitheater. Rows of red seats lined the circular room. Above them, he could see a dome of black glass looking down to the main floor. Precisely in the center sat what looked like a plant in the red earth of Mars. From the room, he could see the green stem, which led up to a purple bulb surrounded by deep green leaves.

"We need to find a way in there!" he shouted at Sara and Anthony.

"What is it?" Sara came running with Anthony tailing her.

"Oh my God," she exclaimed.

"Janelle, can you see this?"

"A little bit, the glass is hard to see through. There's another room but I can't see what's inside it."

"There's a plant!"

"What?!" she exclaimed. "Are you sure?"

"One hundred percent. There's life on Mars! Let Command know!"

"I'll be back, I'm going to transfer the video over and send it back," Janelle replied. Everyone heard her set her headset on the table and run out of the room.

"There has to be another entry point to this place," Noah said, turning to his team.

"Let's head back and see if there's a promising entrance," Sara said.

Noah nodded and they dashed through the door and back up the stairs.

The sun lit up the red sands of Mars as they looked around the base of the rock formation where they were standing.

"I'll go left," Anthony said.

"I'll go right with Sara."

They all nodded and Noah watched Anthony break off in a jog around the corner.

"Noah?" Janelle's voice cracked through his helmet.

"Yes?"

"Command wants to know if you got closer to the plant?"

"We're trying to find another entrance into the structure."

"Okay, I'll let them know. It's also going to be dark soon. If you guys can't find an entrance, you'll have to start making your way back to base."

"Understood," he said as he looked down to the small computer on his arm. "About two hours left," he muttered to himself. "Janelle, please let Sara and Anthony know they have to double time it if we want to gain entrance today."

"Will do," she replied before her voice cut out.

Noah followed the rock circumference. He looked for any crack or hole that would lead him to believe there was an entrance. Though the base of the small mountain was less than a kilometer away, he took his time. More than once he thought there might have been an entrance, but each time he followed a promising lead, there remained no other entrance to the amphitheater.

"I'm going to start heading back to the rover," he radioed Janelle.

"Sounds good. Anthony and Sara were thinking the same thing."

"Damn," he whispered. His hopes had been crushed for the day. Even though they made the discovery of a lifetime, Noah felt like a failure. He wanted to get samples, he wanted to get a closer look to make sure it was actually a plant, and more importantly, he wanted to come back with better news even if he were already bringing back something they never thought they'd find.

The inside of the rover was comfortable. Noah let Anthony drive back while he sat in the back staring off into the distance. The red sand around them swirled up. The glass windows in the back of the rover were a nice addition since the last expedition to this wasteland. It made the rover feel different, better. A simple upgrade made all the difference for the rides to and from the base. Rather than staring at the electronics and white interior, Noah was able to take in the breath-taking views of this alien landscape.

Noah unlatched his helmet from his suit and placed it back on the rack. It was comfortable inside their little station. He pulled himself out of his suit and noticed little stains under his armpits, which he assumed were from the excitement of their discovery.

Janelle was waiting in the main room by the time Noah arrived with the other two. In front of her, she had prepared paperwork about their discovery even though Command had seen the footage.

"It's everyone's favorite time," she announced. They all groaned in unison.

"Better to get it done now than tomorrow morning," Noah said.

They all sat down and scribbled away what they had observed. It was detailed and they all felt exhausted by the time they finished.

"Do we have any other scans of the area?" Noah asked Janelle.

"I ran a few while you were away, but I couldn't find anything on the scans."

"So, no other entrances?" Sara asked.

"Not that any of the scans can see," Janelle retorted.

"Anthony, can you create a small explosive with the chemicals we have here?" Noah turned and asked.

"I mean, I don't think it's a good idea to blow open the glass in an underground structure that we don't know how old it is."

"So you can," Noah said back.

"I can. I'll make the smallest one possible and we can run a cable to it from the rover so no one's inside. But if it goes bad, it could collapse the entrance to the room."

Noah looked over to Janelle. His eyes looked for an answer in hers.

"This is your call, Captain," she replied.

"What would you do?"

"You know what I'd do."

Noah turned to Anthony. "Do it," he said.

"I'll take care of it in the morning before we head back out," Anthony replied.

"And don't tell Command," Noah pointed his finger at Janelle.

She laughed. "Never crossed my mind. I'll send a message that we're hunkering down for the night and found a promising visual."

"Deal," Noah said before he left the room.

His cabin was sparse. He brought the least amount of valuables from Earth among the other members of his team. On his desk sat a cross and a Bible. He wondered if this discovery would change the landscape of religion on Earth. He hoped it wouldn't. He still believed in God, and that they were made in His image. But, having found a place clearly built by sentient life might create turmoil for more zealous individuals. He picked up the cross, pressed it against his lips, and placed it back on the desk.

His bed wasn't uncomfortable, but he missed the comfort of Earth. His home. The friends and family still down there waiting for him to return. He wondered if they looked up to the stars trying to pinpoint the red planet he was exploring. Soon, though, he'd be home. Soon, he thought. He closed his eyes and let sleep take him.

He dreamt of the plant. Green and purple against a red sand. Its roots dug deep, twisting and twining through the barren landscape. Noah watched as form-less beings dug it out of the ground, placed it in a glass container, and transported it to the amphitheater they had discovered. He stood in the room with them as they chanted guttural vowels, arms outstretched. Their heads pointed at the plant in the center of the room. He woke to the sun peering through the small window of his room.

Noah dressed quickly before grabbing breakfast. It was the usual — coffee with dehydrated eggs. Simple. But he enjoyed it. Despite being an astronaut, he was a creature of habit in his normal life. Same routine, same food. But up here, far away from Earth, his routine consisted only of his meals. Sara walked in as he finished the last of the black swill from the pouch.

"You ready?" she asked.

"As soon as I relieve myself, I'll be good to go," he nodded.

"Anthony's prepping the gear right now."

"Janelle working away?"

"As always," Sara replied.

"Okay. I'll meet you two at the rover," he said as he stood up from the table and pushed in his chair.

Noah looked at himself in the mirror of the bathroom. His eyes were drooping, and the stress of the mission, though exciting, was clearly taking its toll on him. The wrinkles near his eyes were deeper, his beard was longer, and the grays were noticeably starting to come in.

The rover was humming when Noah arrived with Sara and Anthony already inside. He walked up the back, and closed the hatch behind him. The secondary seating area had a small white tube strapped to the wall. Noah knew it was the explosive.

"You ready, Captain?" Anthony asked.

"Absolutely," Noah's voice crackled over the comms.

"Then let's blow some shit up!"

Sara laughed. "Janelle, please tell me you aren't live streaming us back to Earth."

"Nope. I am recording your feeds though, at least for documentation sake. Once this is done, and we have the specimen, it'll be better to ask for forgiveness than ask for their permission now."

"Good," Noah said as he sat down and did not strap himself in. He leaned back into the seat and let his eyes close for a moment. The anticipation was welling inside him. Today they'd see it up close. Something perfect, something living, something alien.

The rover came to a stop, and Noah heard the electric whirring of its batteries cease. He stood up and waited for Sara and Anthony to meet him. They grabbed a minimal amount of gear, while Anthony grabbed the explosive.

"You guys ready?" Noah asked.

"Absolutely," Anthony replied, his eyes nervous. Sara nodded.

Noah pressed a button. The ramp opened and lowered onto the sands of Mars.

He watched as Anthony placed the explosive next to the glass barrier separating them from the plant. He tapped away, and plugged a small wire into the top of the container.

"Okay," Anthony said. "It's time to get back to the rover and plug this thing in."

Noah waited and watched as Anthony fed the wire along the ground, looking back at times to make sure he didn't trip as he walked backwards. Noah followed, making sure there were no kinks or tangles in the thin black conductor.

They all stood outside the entrance they had discovered.

"It's now or never, I guess," Sara said.

"Yep," Anthony replied. He walked to the back of the rover, and clipped the wire to an electrical port.

"Would you like to do the honors, Anthony?" Noah asked.

"Absolutely not, Captain. If this is too powerful, I don't want to be the one who destroyed the structure."

"You sound unsure," he replied.

"My measurements are correct, I'm just worried about the stability of the structure."

"Okay, I'll take care of it," Noah said as he walked

back into the rover and sat in the driver's seat. "Ready when you guys are," he announced.

"Janelle, you watching?" Sara asked.

"Feed is crystal clear."

Sara nodded to Noah. He pressed a few buttons above him to override the ignition failsafe for having the ramp open. The rover hummed to life, its electric buzzing filled the air around them. He waited.

There was a small blast. And a slight shaking that came from the tomb. He did not see any dust spurt out from the entrance like it always had in the movies back on Earth.

"Must have been too small to force everything out," he muttered.

"That's it, Captain. Shut the rover down," Anthony announced over the comms as he disappeared from view to disconnect the wire.

Noah turned the rover off, and walked out the back. He pulled a lever, and the ramp lifted back up to its holding position.

"Captain, I know you're eager," Janelle's voice cut through all of their comms. "You can't go in yet."

"How'd you know?"

"You forget I get diagnostics from your suits. Your heart is racing. We need to wait a few minutes to make sure nothing crumbles or collapses."

"Fine," Noah huffed.

"You know she's right," Sara said as she crossed over to Noah.

"Yeah, it's just the anticipation is killing me."

The anticipation is killing us, O Stranger Mine.

"What?" Noah asked.

"I didn't say anything," Sara said confused.

"Sorry, I thought I heard someone talking."

"Maybe just a little lag from the comms."

Noah furrowed his brow. "Yeah, maybe."

They waited almost an hour for anything to happen. Nothing did except for the slow movement of the sun. Noah felt himself growing antsy as they paced around the entrance and back to the rover.

"I think it's safe enough," Janelle said to all of them.

"Let's go," Noah demanded.

The group walked down the red steps. There were tiny fissures, Noah noticed. He wasn't sure they were there the first time they walked into this hidden cathedral. The room was intact, though now it was covered in soot, scraps of metal, and particles of glass that didn't get blown into the amphitheater.

They walked to the blown open glass and looked inside, checking for any damage to the ceiling. There was none as the luminescence from the strange lights lit everything. Noah looked down, the drop from their overlook was maybe two feet. He kicked out the last pieces of glass so they didn't pierce their suits.

Each of them took turns sitting down and hopping to the ground below them. It felt different here, Noah thought, but he wasn't sure what it was. Peculiar. Horrific. Celestial. The words swirled inside his head, but he couldn't decide on the correct adjective.

Anthony walked around the top row to see if there was anything on each other piece of glass that surrounded the amphitheater. Sara followed Noah as he walked down the steps, being careful not to slip on any remnants of debris.

He closed in on the plant, and discovered it was real. Not a statue, nor a monument, but a real, live plant. He knelt beside it and brushed his gloved hand as gently as possible over the green leaves. He dared not touch the purple bulb for fear of breaking it.

Hello, O Stranger mine.

"What?" Noah asked.

"Didn't say anything," Sara said as she looked down on him.

Noah didn't respond. He continued to look over the plant. Its stem reached down into the soil, and he could see little humps coming from the red sand. He assumed it was the roots.

"So close to the surface," he said.

"What is?" Anthony asked.

"The roots. Come take a look."

Anthony came and crouched next to Noah as he pointed to the little hills in the sand.

"Never seen any roots branching that close to the surface before," Anthony said.

"Sara, give me a brush," Noah turned and put his hand out.

Sara reached into a pocket and pulled a fine bristled brush, which she handed over.

He brushed some of the sand away and exposed a root. It was pitch black with purple dots.

Put the sand back. I do not enjoy the cold on my roots.

"No way," Noah mumbled.

"What is it?"

"It's talking to me. The plant is talking to me!"

"Captain, I think you need to get back to base for an examination. Delusions could mean a CO_2 build-up in your suit," Janelle snapped quickly.

"No, I really heard it!"

"Captain, I think Janelle is right," Sara said as she reached down and touched Noah on his shoulder.

She is not right.

Anthony and Sara gasped.

"What is it? Why are all your heart rates skyrocketing?"

"It's talking," Sara and Anthony said in unison.

"That is NOT possible. It breaks all the laws of

nature. It can not SPEAK," Janelle demanded they start using logic.

Noah turned and looked at the other two. "We need to get back to base and find a way to transport this thing safely."

Do not move me from my home.

They all looked at each other as they heard the voice in their heads. They nodded. Noah led the way back to the rover and sat in the driver's seat this time. The electrical humming buzzed and whirred as he pushed the rover as hard as he could.

The airlock hissed as it pressurized for the trio. They all took their helmets off, but left the suits on.

"That is not possible. You all are getting an exam," Janelle demanded.

Noah grabbed her by the shoulders. "We just discovered something entirely alien. We don't know what is or isn't possible beyond our human understanding."

Janelle's eyes widened, then her face contorted with anger.

Before she could speak, Sara broke in. "Put on a suit, Janelle. You can go with them. I'll stay at base and enjoy the oxygen. If there is CO_2 build-up, then I'm already out of the danger zone. I never lost consciousness, so nothing bad can happen if I'm here. I'll pump up the oxygen levels, and you can do a test before you leave."

"Fine, but if I find that your levels are low, then no one leaves and I report to Command."

"Deal," Sara said before Noah could interject.

They all made their way to the medbay. Sara produced her arm after pulling herself from the space-suit. Noah watched as Janelle hooked up an oxygen saturation meter to Sara's arm. She then proceeded to take her blood pressure. He saw on the screen that everything came back within optimal range. Even though he knew deep down that nothing was wrong, he still breathed a sigh of relief.

"See, we weren't imagining it," he said.

Janelle shot him a look but did not say a word.

"Suit up, Janelle," Sara said as she unhooked the machine from her arm. "I can handle it here."

"Fine," she retorted as she stormed off.

Sara crossed the room and stood in front of Noah. "We just made the discovery of a generation. Maybe the biggest discovery of humanity's entire existence," she whispered.

"I know. Janelle still doesn't believe us. But, she'll find out soon," he said as Janelle walked back in.

"We need to leave now if we still want the sunlight on our way back," Janelle demanded. Her helmet carried under her right arm.

Noah patted Sara on the arm, then nodded to Anthony, who remained quiet.

The rover trudged on, and Noah felt himself getting restless with the half-hour ride back to the structure. No one spoke, but he had so many questions to ask. Though, he felt silence was the best option until Janelle discovered they weren't losing their minds. Noah put the rover in park and stopped the batteries.

"This place is a wonder," Janelle said as they descended the staircase.

"It only gets better. I wish I understood where the power source for the lights was coming from," Noah replied.

They continued down the steps until they came to the room with the shattered glass.

"It's so different in person than seeing this on a screen."

"We kicked the glass out. You can sit, then hop down," Noah said as they approached the viewing for the amphitheater.

"It's so odd seeing that thing from here."

"Come take a closer look." Noah held out his hand and helped Janelle down from the ledge. They walked down the stairs and felt the Mars sand again beneath their feet.

Welcome back.

"Did you hear that?" Noah said excitedly.

"I heard nothing," Janelle's voice cracked.

"Me either," Anthony intruded.

Noah turned back and crouched in front of the plant. "I brought someone else for you to meet."

I see this.

"She doesn't think you're really speaking to us."

I wouldn't either if I were her.

"Why's that?" Noah asked. There was no response.

"Janelle come over here and try talking to it."

Noah saw Janelle roll her eyes behind her helmet as she stepped closer and crouched down.

"Hello," she said with an attitude.

"Did it say anything?" Noah asked.

"No, it didn't. You guys are fucking losing it just like I said," she snapped.

You all should be more excited.

Janelle blinked.

"You heard that," Noah said flatly.

Janelle tilted her head. Her eyes said she was trying to understand what just happened. Something logical or scientific for the disruption in her knowledge.

"How long have you been here?" Noah asked. "Please, talk to us all as I ask questions."

Okay. I've been here longer than your kind has existed.

"How do you know how long we've existed?" Noah asked.

Because I can communicate in your language. I understand you.

"What does that mean?" Janelle shrieked.

I do not feel like elaborating.

"Okay, hear me out," Anthony's voice hung over the comms. "Suspend belief for a moment. This thing is telepathic; we can agree on that. So, what if it's able to read our minds without us knowing. Like, really read our minds. All the knowledge we have between us, even when we don't use it?"

"Interesting hypothesis," Noah said.

He's the smart one of you three.

Anthony laughed. "But where does it store all the knowledge? I don't see it having a brain, nor a place for synapses to be firing."

Your human understanding can never come to a scientific understanding of me. I am evolutionarily better than you. Not some mere ape who has discovered a way to travel between planets in its own solar system.

"What if this isn't actually communicating to us? What if there's a broadcast somewhere on the planet?" Janelle interjected a hypothesis.

"Maybe. I could also see—," Noah was cut off.

Despite the reasonable hypothesis, Janelle. I'd like to inform you that you're wrong. Blatantly, in fact.

"I still withhold belief."

Your father died when you were twenty-four. The plant spoke to all of them.

Noah turned back to Janelle. Her eyes wide, like a deer in headlights, or an owl staring into the darkness she wished to forget. Something depressing was welling up inside of her, something not forgotten, but something repressed.

Does that help you understand a little bit better?

"I'll be in the rover," she said. Her tone was angry, not because she didn't already know what had happened all those years ago, but because something had probed her mind, discovered that kernel of truth, and used it to embarrass her.

"Janelle, wait," Noah said as he reached out, but she was already running up the stairs to climb back through the busted glass.

"Just let her go," Anthony said. "I think we got enough information for today. We can radio to Command and get some directives for our next expedition here."

"I guess you're right." Noah turned back to the plant. He reached out and let his gloved fingers brush gently against the leaves.

Please, do not touch me. I do not enjoy the feeling.

"I only meant it as a kind gesture. A way to be non-hostile."

If you truly were non-hostile, you would not have blown open that glass and invaded my home. You are a brute, no different than your neanderthal ancestors. Your evolution has failed you and your belief to be something more—something better—is a delusion.

"Let's go," Noah said as he turned back to Anthony, who nodded in agreement.

They drove back in the rover with its microelectronics whirling and buzzing away. They did not speak, but every chance Noah had to look over at Janelle, he took. There was still something in her eyes. Something he couldn't exactly put his finger on. Not anger, nor malice, not a sadness either. She seemed empty, like all of her beliefs about the universe and how it worked had gone out the window, and now she was just an empty human who had nothing left to grip on to.

Noah stopped the rover as gently as he could. Anthony had already opened up the ramp by the time he unlatched the door to the rear compartment. They walked inside and listened to the hiss of the airlock. Janelle took her helmet off gently, then slipped out of her spacesuit. She let it hang near the pressurized door before walking off. Her footsteps made no noise as she left Noah and Anthony in the room together. They heard the door to her bedroom close, and Noah could have sworn he heard a small whimper come from the other side as soon as it did.

"Let's go talk to Sara," Anthony said as he put a hand on Noah's shoulder.

"Yeah. Best to just let Janelle be right now," he replied lowly.

"Exactly."

They walked to the main room. Sara was waiting, sitting in the chair overlooking the terminals of their feeds. She was replaying every video that had just been transmitted back.

"Find anything interesting?" Noah asked.

"Not really. Nothing that we haven't already predetermined. I'm getting ready to upload these to Command. Then we can ask for forgiveness. I think tomorrow we need to dig that thing up as carefully as possible and bring it back here to be examined. I already put together a large specimen pod for it. We can fill another with the dirt from the amphitheater and bring that back to re-plant it. Then Janelle can take a sample and see if it's the same dirt and sand that's around the base."

"Sounds good to me," Noah said.

"I can do the sample work," Anthony interjected. "I think Janelle needs some alone time for a bit."

"Yeah..." Sara replied. "Didn't expect that as a reply."

"None of us did. But I think the plant proved its point. It really can read our minds." Noah looked down to Sara. "True history in the making right now."

"And trauma," Sara said.

Anthony let out a chuckle. "I'm sorry," he said. "It's true. This thing can't go back to Earth yet. It'll cause too many issues being able to read everyone's mind who comes into contact with it."

"We don't even know how far its range is."

"Or what else it's capable of," Sara said quickly.

"Alright, then let's get these carriers ready to move the specimen, Anthony. Sara, let Command know we're moving it to the enclosed section of the lab. Send them all of our footage and let them know we have had no signs of illness. Please include your readouts for them."

"On it, Captain," she replied.

Noah walked with Anthony to the lab. They talked of nothing, but each knew the other was thinking of the impact this would have on humanity when it was finally announced. Utter panic. They each worried about it, but in the same breath, they each reveled in the idea of something sentient being discovered so close to their home.

Noah prepped a few small containers while he let Anthony work on piecing together a larger one.

"Do you think this thing needs CO_2 to survive?"

"I'd say so," Noah said back.

"Okay, I'll reconfigure one of our extra PBAs to produce the same atmospheric makeup."

"Good, we need to configure the atmosphere in the holding cell of the lab as well. I want to do that before we leave so we can transport it as quickly as possible to lessen the risk of destroying it."

"I'll take care of that," Sara's voice cut in behind them.

"All done?"

"All done. I didn't want to wait for a response from Command. I also conveniently left out the mental state of Janelle for the time being. Don't need anyone telling us we can't do this."

Noah smiled. "Thank you for that."

"Like we said, better to ask forgiveness than ask for permission."

They toiled away. Noah had set up three containers for soil and loaded them into the rover, while Anthony finished rigging together a breathing apparatus to a larger container for the specimen. Sara had quickly set the correct atmosphere in the lab, and then they called it a day. Tomorrow would be the big moment. They all waited with bated breath.

Noah had hardly slept, the adrenaline for the mission coursed through him, and he heard the beeping of a message from Command coming from the other side of his door. He purposely ignored it.

When they all met in the mess room, Janelle was still locked in her room.

"Should we invite her?" Sara asked.

"I'll do it," Noah nodded as he walked off and knocked on her door.

"Janelle, we're going to begin transport on the specimen. Would you like to come?"

There was silence, then a brief knocking of feet beyond the door. It opened. Her eyes were bloodshot, and bags had developed under them. Noah knew Janelle hadn't slept a wink.

"I'll stay here and watch," she said.

"Thank you," he said as he reached out and put his hand on her shoulder. She did not pull away. "We told Command what we're doing. There's a message at the terminal but we haven't listened to it."

"Understood, Captain."

Noah met up with Sara and Anthony by the airlock. They were already suited up. He put his on, and they opened the door to the Mars landscape. The sand crunched beneath their feet, and in the distance the peaks of mountains watched over them.

"Let's do this," he said as he sat in the front of the rover and turned the machine on. It hummed along the rolling sands. Noah admired the foreign landscape as they drove on. It reminded him of the time he had visited Colorado. At the base of the Rockies he sat in the sand waiting for the sun to drop so he could see the night sky under the full moon. It had lit up everything around him, and the brown sand turned blue with its iridescent glow. Thinking of it, he wanted to come out of the base when the sun set on Mars so he could see the alien landscape in anything other than a bright sky.

The rover came to a stop, and they all unloaded from the back. Noah carried the large container for the specimen, while Anthony and Sara made multiple trips back to the rover for the soil collectors. Each step he took was deliberate. He did not want to risk dropping their rigged container and have the day be a waste.

Noah passed the container down to Anthony as they entered the amphitheater.

"Okay," he said as they approached the plant. "Let's start digging up the roots and I'll start digging down near the base of this thing."

Do not move me.

"I'm sorry. We only want to understand you better."

Anything you learn from your science experiments I could simply tell you.

Noah ignored the statement and began digging. The sand parted under the small metal shovel, and Noah began making piles next to his right leg, which looked like ant hills.

I will not take this lightly, O Transgressor Mine.

"Please, just let us work. We'll bring you back."

I know that is a lie. You will send me off to your space station for further testing. From there, you do not know what will happen to me. I may become dust from fire, or your kind may try to create another version of me. Though, you do not know which.

Noah stopped digging as the plant continued to talk. He felt a small pain in his head, like something was probing deep into his subconscious, pulling out thoughts he was not currently thinking, but had deep down and did not entertain. He breathed deep, and continued his work.

"We're done exposing the roots," Anthony said.

"Affirmative. Get a soil sample near the roots, and then another on the other side of the amphitheater."

Anthony nodded and began scooping Mars dirt into his containers. Noah watched as he pulled a marker out, and drew a line on the glass of one.

"This one is root samples," he said.

"Got it," Janelle cracked through all of their comms.

"Okay, guys. I'm ready to begin moving the specimen into the container," Noah said as Anthony finished locking the smaller ones with samples.

I said do not move me.

They all ignored the voice in their heads and gently pulled the plant from the ground and placed it into the container roots first. Anthony made sure there was enough of the Martian sand in the bottom of the container. Still, it barely fit as its black roots started to twist and turn as they transported it. Noah swore he saw it try to wrap itself around one of their arms, but chalked it up to their movements.

You will pay for this transgression, it said as they locked the lid and began moving all of their samples back to the rover.

Noah sighed with relief when he realized it was still alive.

"Okay, when we get back, we fill the lab with soil from outside, and then replant it."

Anthony and Sara both nodded.

The ride back was mostly quiet. The specimen was on Sara's lap as she was sitting in the front of the rover.

It has been so long since I've felt the sun upon me. Glorious in all its might. I still hate you all.

"Why were you locked away?" Noah asked.

There was a brief moment of silence.

I was revered by the people who used to reside here. I was their God.

"What happened to them?"

You see it. This once fertile place dried up. There was no way for them to continue on this planet. They eventually all died off.

"And their bodies?" Noah turned to look at the container.

Me.

"What do you mean?"

There was no response.

The rover came to a stop, and Anthony exited first to get the lab set up for processing. Noah grabbed the containers and loaded them into the airlock while Sara waited with hers in tow. It hissed and pressurized. They all moved quickly. Noah and Anthony unloaded the dirt into a holding container. Sara waited until it was time to begin.

They unlatched their specimen's cell, and gently pulled it out. Their hands getting in the way of each other at times. Noah dug a small pit and placed the stem into it while Sara held the plant up. Anthony dug small ravines and laid the roots into them before covering them again. They closed the container, flicked a few switches and pressed a few buttons. There was a hiss as the atmosphere inside matched that outside on Mars. They all breathed a sigh of relief and pulled their helmets off.

"Okay, let's get dressed and talk to Command," Noah said.

They both nodded as they disappeared to hang their suits and change into more comfortable clothes.

Noah was worn out from the excitement. His eyes reflected in the mirror of his room. They had bags upon bags dragging down his cheekbones. He rubbed them, then turned on the sink and splashed a little of the precious water onto them. It would be okay, he thought. The water would get recycled and put back into the system. He changed his shirt and walked to the command room.

"Any word?" he asked.

"They aren't happy with us whatsoever."

"Oh well, time to ask for forgiveness," he shrugged.

Noah walked up to the computer, and started a video recording.

"Command, this is Captain Noah Jackson. We have secured the specimen, and limited damage to the underground structure. We will begin testing as soon as possible, and begin relaying our findings. As you know by now, we believe the specimen has the ability to communicate telepathically. We have completed routine testing on every member of the crew for hallucinations and bodily function, along with swapping out a member as a control. Discovery showed that the new member was able to communicate with the plant as well. Tomorrow we plan to probe, sample, and look at the cellular makeup of the plant and relay our findings. On behalf of the crew, I apologize for going against direct orders, and any repercussions should be brought down directly on myself, as I ordered the rest of the crew to follow my instruction and my instruction alone."

Not half bad, Noah. Not half bad.

Noah blinked, and came to a realization.

"Holy shit," he said as he ended the recording and sent it back to Earth.

"What?" Sara asked.

"I heard it."

"Yeah, we all heard it."

"No, I mean…I heard the thing talking to me in here. We never heard it when we left the structure."

"Wait," Sara said.

"Yes. Exactly. We need to get a sample of that glass. Maybe it was stopping its ability to talk somehow. Or at least limiting how far out it could reach."

"Okay. Okay," Sara said as she began to pace.

"Tomorrow, though. Anthony you're on it," Noah said as he pointed to him.

"Absolutely, Captain." He nodded in assent.

"For now, let's get some rest and wait for a reply from Command. I'm sure they'll be less than pleased. Maybe a court martial is in order," Noah laughed.

"Luckily they can't drag you back to Earth just yet," Anthony said.

"What do we have?" Sara asked.

"To send a manned mission? Without seeing trajectories, I'd say the usual nine month period. They'd never be able to send the crew from the NSS to us," Noah replied.

"Ha. Well I guess we got you a little bit longer," Sara smiled.

Noah nodded and finally relaxed. "Okay, I'm going to my room to get some sleep."

They didn't say anything back this time. Only then did they realize how tired they all were. The crew stretched and yawned, and all retired.

Noah sat in his room, looking around at what he now called home. It was the great journey of humanity. To sail among the stars and discover a lost civilization. To discover a lasting remnant, not bones of something forgotten, but something entirely different. Something that could only be dreamed of in the tomes of science fiction. He smiled to himself, laid back into his bed, and closed his eyes.

"To be a greek god," he whispered.

You don't even know which one you'd be.

Noah's smile turned sour. He didn't. Was he knowledgeable, curious, or something different. His mythology was weak, but he felt himself on a pedestal nonetheless. Yet, the specimen had just taken that joy from him within a moment's notice.

The sun rose over the Mars landscape, and Noah had slept through his alarm. He knew he dreamed, but did not remember anything except the feeling of fright. He sat up in bed and wiped the sweat from his forehead before placing his feet on the floor. It was cool to the touch.

How I long to feel that same coolness.

He ignored the voice in his head, and walked out of his room without changing his clothes. Sara was already at the computer typing away on a report.

"Good morning, Captain."

"Morning," Noah said as he rubbed the crust from his eyes. They felt like pieces of sand against his eyelids until they eventually broke off and fell to the floor. "Any word from Command?"

"They're extremely unhappy with you, but you haven't been court-martialed. They want us to begin our experiments. They're arranging for us to send the specimen to the NSS for further testing."

"Of course they are," he grumbled. "What about Anthony?"

"He already has a sample of the glass, and is on his way back."

"Janelle?"

Sara shook her head and her lips made the classic face where they pulled taut against her teeth.

Noah sighed. "Okay, let me get dressed then I'll head in and begin some tests."

Sara nodded and turned back to the screen in front of her.

"Why do they need to take the greatest discovery from us the second we find it?"

That's what your kind does. You are thieves.

"We are not thieves. We just want to understand you better. We want to understand what was *here* better."

O Naivety Mine, you know that your kind has always done this.

"And how would you know that?"

I know everything you all know. And when I meet those on your Naval Space Station, I will know everything they also know.

"A mind reader."

Took you long enough.

Noah didn't respond as he opened the door to his room and got dressed. His clothes felt stiff today, scratchy even. There was a discomfort he couldn't quite put his finger on. Like something in the air was creating friction in his head. He walked to the lab.

"Sara, I'm here," he announced.

"I got eyes on you, Captain. Anthony has also returned and will be bringing the sample in."

"Heard," he responded. Noah walked over the container holding the plant. He put his arms through two holes, and let his hands slip into the gloves attached to them.

"I'm pulling a sample from the root now," he said as he lifted a syringe with a microscopic needle. He pressed it into part of a black root that was exposed from the sand they had installed.

This is unpleasant.

"I'm sorry," he said as he pulled the syringe out, and placed the sample on a small piece of glass. He repeated the process with the stem, one of the leaves, and the flower bud.

I do not wish for you to touch me, O Sadist Mine.

"It's not meant for harm. I promise."

I'm sure that's exactly what that Nazi doctor said to his experiments as well.

Noah thought about it for a moment, then pushed the spiraling from his head. He felt guilt, but continued with the samples.

Anthony arrived as Noah was finishing. He carried a piece of glass and placed it on an examination table opposite Noah. Noah nodded to him as he pulled his hands from the gloves.

Noah looked at his slides under a microscope. The cells moved sporadically even though they were no longer attached to its host.

"Interesting. I see no cell death occurring. In fact, it even looks like they're replicating."

"Replicating?"

"Yeah, some are attaching themselves to others and forming larger cells."

"Do you see any cell division?"

"Not yet," Noah replied.

"Keep them in a stable environment and we'll continue experiments in a few hours."

"Will do," he said as he pulled the slide, and placed it in a small compartment underneath the container that housed their specimen.

You will pay.

"What?"

You will pay for this.

Noah blew off the voice in his head and walked back to the main room where Sara stood. She was watching the computer in front of her.

"I've sent a message back to Command with the new information. We should receive a response within the hour."

"Good. I'm going to grab something to eat while Anthony checks the glass. I'll check on Janelle."

Noah walked away, and before he reached the mess hall, he knocked on Janelle's door.

"Are you okay in there?" he asked.

There was a sniffling sound on the other side.

"Come on, Janelle. We're at the precipice of the greatest discovery in human history. You should be excited about this."

Noah waited. There was a slapping of feet on the floor before her door opened. Janelle's eyes were blood-shot, and the bags underneath them showed she had barely slept.

"I am excited. But I'm terrified, Captain. That thing hasn't stopped talking to me since we got back. I hear it every second. Speaking to me. Telling me all my darkest secrets. All my insecurities. The worst things I've ever done. I can't fucking take it." She started crying hysterically as she sat down on the floor and threw her head into her hands. "I can't fucking take it," she wailed.

Noah bent down beside her and put his arms around her. "Hey, hey. It's okay. It's been talking to me, too. But we're going to figure out what it is. Command should be receiving our findings now."

Janelle sniffed, then wiped her nose on her arm. "What'd you find?"

"The cells aren't dying after we retrieve them from the specimen. They start to bunch together and form larger cells. Sara has us waiting to see if cell division starts."

Janelle's eyes widened. "No. That can't be. We can't have another one of those things here. We just can't."

"Shh. It's okay. Command wants us to send it to the NSS. I'm not happy about it, but it'll be gone soon."

Just as Noah spoke the words, Sara's voice came over the intercom.

"Captain, please report back. I have received word from Command."

"You coming?" he asked Janelle as he stood up and stretched out a hand.

"Yeah, I'll come," she said as she tried to wipe tears from her face.

The walk back was brief, and Noah had forgotten that he was hungry. Anthony was waiting next to Sara as they both arrived. Neither said a word to Janelle, only nodded.

"What is it?"

"They want the specimen sent to the NSS immediately."

"How immediately?"

"We have forty-eight hours to get it on a pod and launch it. They say there's a storm brewing off to the West. It'll hit us in four days and last a day or so. It isn't particularly strong, but it'll disrupt communications for the time-being."

Noah sighed. "Okay. Then let's grab a meal together, check on our sample, and begin the process of loading this thing."

This is what I spoke of. Your kind will never accept me.

Noah didn't respond.

Noah ate slowly. Surrounded by Janelle, Sara, and Anthony, he felt defeated. Command had sent the order down to stop their experiments and get the specimen closer to home. He couldn't delay it, though he wanted to. This order wasn't up for debate.

"You know what we have to do," he said.

Sara and Anthony both nodded. Noah looked over to Janelle. For the first time since they went on their expedition, she finally smiled.

"Thank God," she muttered as she started to cry again.

"I know. I know," Noah said. "I'm disappointed, but I know you'll find relief in this."

It's the last relief you all will ever know.

"Let's finish up, and start prepping this thing."

The rest of the crew nodded in assent and ate quietly.

Noah was the first one in the lab. He had set down the container and placed soil in it for the specimen to rest in. Anthony, Sara, and Janelle all came to watch as he shuffled around the lab.

Finally, he began the process of moving the plant. He gently brushed the dirt away with his gloved hands inside the container, then he opened the panel on the side.

He gently lifted the specimen from the tray. Its roots slowly wriggled then found his wrist. They twisted and gripped his exposed skin.

"Interesting," he muttered.

"What is it?" Sara asked.

"It's able to move its roots. They wrapped around my arm."

"I'll pass that message along to Command. You're wearing gloves right?"

"No," Noah said. Before Sara could reply, he confirmed he would go through decontamination.

"Don't be so eager next time. I won't mention your dcon to Command."

"Thanks for that," he replied.

You feel so alien. Warm. Your skin is coarse and your hair disgusts me.

"I'm already going through dcon, so I'm going to feel the roots, bulb, and leaves," he announced. Before Sara could put her opinion in, Noah felt all the smoothness of the plant. It was like silk. Smooth. Soft. Fragile. As Noah reached for the bulb, the specimen opened up, and a small black cloud of particles released into the air.

"Vent the area!" he yelled as he shook the plant to the floor, and ran for an oxygen mask. As soon as he got it on, the room turned red, and alarms blared. He watched as the black dust quickly was vacated from the lab. Just as quickly as the room turned red, the lights turned back to their soft white glow.

"Check the specimen. We need to see if we killed it with that stunt," Sara's voice crackled over the intercoms.

Noah walked over to the plant, and slowly picked it up.

You hurt me.

"It's still here. It spoke to me."

There was an audible sigh from Sara. "Okay, good. Get it into the pod."

Noah worked quickly, keeping his oxygen mask over his face. He placed the specimen in the pod, covered its roots with soil, and for good measure, he took a small piece of the glass from the amphitheater and placed it at the bottom. He locked the pod, and went to decontamination.

You'll pay. Your entire kind will pay. You wound me. Abuse me. And stuff me into claustrophobic places.

Noah ignored the voice as he stood in the shower. Then there was a quick vent, before the UV lights clicked on. Noah stood there for a few minutes, letting the emptiness of his mind take over.

"Anthony, start moving the specimen," he announced. "I'm going to run dcon a few more times to be safe."

"Understood, Captain."

By the time Noah had returned to Sara, Anthony was already at the table waiting beside her and Janelle.

"Launch in 2 minutes," Sara said.

"I thought we had more time?"

"Command said the storm is picking up speed and strengthening. We're launching ASAP."

"Alright, so we'll be hunkered down for a while."

"Yep."

"I'm going to get a better look out the window at the launch," he said.

"Me, too," Anthony and Janelle said in unison.

They all jogged to the far side of the colony. Just inside the mess hall, there was a small window that gave them all a perfect view of the small vehicle holding their discovery.

"Five, four, three, two, one, and launch," Sara's voice announced.

The thrusters kicked in. A billow of smoke and dust filled up beneath the vehicle. It slowly lifted off the ground, and then began its arch into the atmosphere.

You're welcome to die here. The last words hung in Noah's head. He wondered if anyone else had heard it. As he turned to look at the other two, he noticed the tears in Janelle's eyes and the blank look on Anthony's face.

"What's that supposed to mean?" Anthony said.

"I don't know," Noah replied. He coughed. Then he coughed harder until he felt light headed. He tucked his mouth into his elbow as he sat down against the wall. When he pulled his arm away, he noticed his white shirt was covered in blood. And in the stain of red, he saw black flecks. For a moment, he could have sworn they moved.

I want to feel my roots burrow through your eyes until

they taste your brain—that sweet nectar I live for. I want to embody your skin, feel every thought as you lay there whimpering. Begging me to end your life, knowing that I hold the key to your end and finding that I will not let it come.

Through the window, Noah could see the pod breaching the Mars atmosphere. He looked down to his arm, and could have sworn he saw one of the small black flecks lift from the blood on his shirt and drift off into the base.

A NIGHTMARE OF SAND
SEATTLE OUTSKIRTS, 2249

"Father, life has forgotten me."
The sun will die before your heart stops beating and your
soul is brought peace.

THE DARK CLOUD at the edge of the world continued on until it sank below the horizon. Tey let the winds blow through her hair. Her hair was only a few shades lighter than the sands around her. She felt the wind cutting through her torn jeans, held together with duct tape just above the knee on the right side and under her left ass cheek. Her blue eyes gazed into the distance. She pulled the red bandana from her neck and tied it to cover her mouth and nose, then produced a black one which she wrapped around her forehead to keep her hair out of her eyes.

The sand would be on her soon, and with it everything terrible that came along. Her goggles were old, metal with a clean black strap and slightly tinted glass. A gift from her dad. Back before the dirt and sand buried him in the city with nameless ghosts. She turned to leave and wondered what hidden monsters lurked this time.

Tey wandered back to the bazaar at the center of town. Draperies hung all around her, colored crimson and blue for the local gang running this area.

"Anything good?" she asked one of the vendors closing up shop.

"Always got something good, but now's not the time. The clouds are coming."

Tey nodded. Once the clouds arrived, the storms would cover the entire place. It was always the same. Hide in the old building of a past civilization until the storms passed, then come out on top of the new dirt and sand it had deposited. Rebuild. Then do it all over again until the next cloud.

"They're coming more frequently, you know," the vendor said to her.

"I know," she said looking off into the distance between the steel girders. *This place is going to be nothing more than dreams of sand,* she thought to herself.

"Well, are you going to stand there or are you going to help?" He demanded an answer.

"I don't work for free."

Tey left before her reply warranted a fight. *I need to find shelter, then get moving before the raiders come through. Daft bastards, riding behind the storms to pillage anything that isn't buried, killing anyone who survives,* Tey's inner dialogue started to kick in. She looked up to the sky. It had become hazy as small crystals of sand began to float between her and the sun. *Soon,* she thought as she found her way to an old skyscraper. *This one's running out of floors to shack up on.* She looked and saw maybe twenty floors left before there was nowhere else for them to go. Before stepping inside, she took one last look behind her at the oncoming storm. *This one is moving fast.* It had already closed half the distance between the bazaar and the horizon. *Less than an hour and we'll be in the shit.* Her left hand fell to her hip at the old metal pipe taped together. It wasn't much, but it carried enough weight to keep people away from her. *Just more inherited gear. Just keep me alive, that's all I ask,* she prayed to herself.

Tey hustled up the clanky steps until she found her room which still had glass windows. The tint of her goggles made the world dark, and the dirt had already begun to block out the sun. She closed a brown wooden door behind her and sat facing the windows. She watched as the storm rode in on silver wind that howled and slammed into the windows. *Any moment now*, she thought. She tied her bandana tighter, and pulled her arms into her jacket only after she had stuffed her hands into the pockets.

Outside the small flecks of dirt and sand began to pelt the glass with little tinks. As the wind whipped, shaking the building, the small tinks turned into thunderous crashes as hundreds of small particles collided with the barrier protecting Tey. She could no longer see any sunlight as the room grew dark and the brown masses shut out the light. If she waved her hand in front of her face, she knew she'd never see it. *Best to keep the goggles on and wait. If anything breaks, at least my eyes will be spared—assuming I live.* Tey ran her fingers over one another and could have sworn the scars on her hands were burning from the memories. She took a deep breath, not wanting to go down that road and relive those moments. "Not now," she whispered.

Soon, my child, a voice that was not her own appeared in her head.

"What was that?" she asked no one.

She closed her eyes but it made no difference. The world was dark now as the sands and dirt piled up outside. Another gust pelted the glass and Tey could have sworn that the building shifted beneath her. *Please don't crumble, don't fall like so many of your brothers and sisters have,* she pondered. She pulled her knees close to her chest, wrapped her arms around them, and lay the left side of her head on her forearms for comfort. She knew she wouldn't fall asleep, but she tried anyway, hoping that the darkness now surrounding her would trick her mind into getting rest. Another gust and then a crash as glass shattered on the same floor Tey sat up. She heard it sprinkling on the ground. The wind whipped through the hallway and searched for any nook and cranny to burrow into. She heard it creep under the door to her room. It was a thin whisper, enticing someone to open up so it could flood in.

Tey sat as the wind blew through her floor. Beneath the howls and gusts slamming against closed doors, she could have sworn she heard an incessant chanting. *Please, not yet, let me get through this night before they come,* she pleaded. The men and women riding pale beasts, cloaked in torn rags made of human skin. They were a nightmare to behold and a worse one to have the displeasure of living though. She felt her scars flaring up from the memories of the only time she met them.

There was a stabbing from the sand tearing into her skin as it cut down to her muscles. She screamed as the husks of people held her down and kept her arm out the window of the house she hid in. They had soulless black eyes and tendrils which ran down their body and across the landscape. Her father came running that time and killed them all before they knew what happened. He picked her up, and they ran. It was the same dream every time. Her brain had blocked out the rest.

She flexed her fingers and listened. If there was chanting, it had stopped. *Maybe it was just my ears playing tricks on me.* But her gut knew she was right. Her father had told her to believe in her senses when her world was dark. "Train your ears and your nose when you're as still as a stone," he said. "They'll be the only things you can trust in the dark."

Still as stone. Do not even become a whisper in the night, the words of her father played in her head. Tey pulled the collar of her shirt up and used it to cover the lower half of her neck as she consciously breathed through her nose. Slow steady breaths filled her lungs and she exhaled all the toxic air from her body. *In. Slow. Out. Slow. Control. Do not let them hear you. Still as stone. Do not even become a whisper in the night,* she thought.

The night slogged on but eventually turned to day. With the last rays of darkness dissipating into the horizon, so did the wind stop blowing and the sand stop falling. Tey uncovered her face and lifted her goggles, which tinted the world around her. It took a moment for her eyes to adjust to the new yet familiar brightness. Even though it stung something deep inside her skull, she welcomed it. Tey stood up and watched a thin film of dust fall off of her. For a moment, she could have sworn it held its shape, like a perfect copy of herself had just fallen to the floor.

Tey arrived outside and made her way to the bazaar. It was littered with people. There was a low hum as they all spoke at the same time. None of it was intelligible. As she got closer, Tey realized she was not crazy. There had been visitors. The bazaar was torn apart. Bright colored flags had been torn and littered the pale colored ground. It was a disaster. Luminous red patches looked like fresh blood, and deep blues reminded her of deep puddles of water as she watched people trying to salvage whatever they could amidst the wreck that had become their tiny lives. As she walked through, she found a small crowd murmuring in a circle. In the middle lay a plant. It was green with small tendrils coming from it. Its buds were a dark purple, something she had rarely seen except in old photos in the high rises. As she stood staring at it with the rest, the crowd slowly got bigger around her.

Too many people in one spot. Too much talking, she thought.

That's right, Tey. There are too many people talking, the other voice in her head had returned.

"Who's there?" she asked aloud.

For a moment, no one acknowledged what she had said. But, as her words hung in the air, the men and women around her dressed in tattered garb and exposed skin began to eyeball her like a mad woman.

Tey sulked back through the large crowd brushing shoulders with raw skin and dull clothes. She rubbed her head.

"Maybe all that sand is getting to me. I should sleep."

Yes, you should, O Sleeper Mine.

"Fuck, I'm losing it," she muttered but this time the voice in her head did not reply.

Her bedroom was exactly how she left it. Blanket neatly tucked into her cot, her clothes folded neatly just as her father taught her. His voice rang in her memories: "It was always better to leave a neat home to come back to if the world outside was a disorganized mess." She took off her boots without untying the laces and collapsed on top of the wool blanket with ornate its embroidery.

Her dreams were vivid. Men and women dancing in the sand storms. Their animals sullen and bony as they carried weight. They disappeared, then Tey found herself in the rundown building. Her arm outside of the window as the sand tore at her skin. She tried to scream, but nothing came out. She prayed for her father, but this time he never came.

Tey woke in a sweat. Her hair matted to her forehead. The pits of her arms soaked through her shirt, which peeled from the blanket as she stood up. Outside is was dark again. She crossed the room and lit a candle, illuminating her room. The fire danced and twirled against the shadows as she pulled her clothes off her sweaty body and laid them in a pile near the doorway.

"Better get those washed," she said as she pulled out a new shirt and soft pants.

Tey sat at her desk and looked out onto the city. It was clear outside, and the moon lit up the world for her to see. The sand had turned shades of blue and purple under its glow. She groaned sitting there, realizing she was still exhausted and her body ached in places she hadn't felt for a while.

Her bed caressed her as she pulled the blanket to the side and sulked back in. The candle still burned, but she didn't worry about it. The wax would pool along the metal base and snuff itself out.

Sweet dreams, O Dreamer Mine, the voice whispered as Tey's eyes closed and she drifted into that other plane of existence.

Tey woke to the clashing of glass. She darted up to find her window had been broken and dust began to pour in from another sandstorm. She threw on a pair of jeans and a t-shirt then ran out of the room. The hallway was littered with people, all of them looking for wood to board up their windows.

"Where did this one come from?" she asked an elderly woman shuffling through.

"No idea, honey. The scouts didn't even give us a warning. This one seems to have come from nowhere."

"Okay, stay here," Tey said. "I'll find something to help seal your room." She put her hand on the woman's shoulder before jogging down the hallway through the thrall of people.

There was already a line near the supply station. Luckily, it was clearing out fast. People were allowed two pieces to put up, and if they needed more, they could return.

Tey grabbed the wood without saying a word and ran back to her floor. The woman was waiting, and Tey walked into her room.

Inside was a disaster. Sand had piled up and Tey knew she'd have to help clear it out for the woman after she handled her own broken window.

"You have any nails?"

"No, just some left over tape."

"It'll have to do. Hold this here for me, and I'll tape it," Tey said as she grabbed a chair to stand on. The sand still seeped in, but she had slowed it to a thin trickle. It would have to do.

"I have to go take care of my place now," she said as she put the duct tape down on the woman's desk. Beside it sat a plant. Green with deep purple bulbs.

"How'd you get this? I saw it outside."

"A plant my grandson brought back from a scavenging trip. It's really beautiful isn't it?"

"In a weird way, I guess." Tey didn't enjoy the look. It was sickly, but she didn't want to insult the woman.

I'm beautiful, aren't I?

"What?" Tey asked.

"I said, isn't it beautiful?"

"You didn't hear that?"

"Hear what?"

"That talking," Tey said.

"It's just us, sweetie. I think you're imagining things."

Tey shook her head. "No, I definitely heard someone talking."

The elderly woman looked weirdly at Tey. "I think you should go get some more wood, I'll wait outside to help you put it in place."

"Yeah," Tey said. "Thank you. I'll be back shortly."

Tey returned to find the woman waiting outside her room. They went inside and Tey pounded a few nails she had into the wood. It was a better seal than the woman's room.

"What's your name anyway?"

"Gertrude," the woman said.

"Thank you, Gertrude. I'm—"

"Tey. I knew your father."

Tey was taken aback. She led a quiet life, keeping to herself any chance she could. No one spoke to her about her father or the mother she never got to know.

"I-I-I'm sorry. How do you know my father?" she asked, looking perplexed.

"He was a good man, helped a lot of us during the journey here. Back when we were living in the old woods."

"He briefly talked about it, that the sands came when he was young, and that they drove everyone to these old cities."

"Yes, dear. Our water left us with the coming sand. We needed to come here. We heard the rumors that there was water in abundance. That people had tapped into the old technology."

"I'm guessing it was true," Tey said.

"True enough. We have water here. If we stayed in those woods, we would have certainly died."

"How long ago was that?"

"Oh," the woman said as she scratched her chin. "Maybe fifty or so."

Tey did quick math in her head. "My dad was really young. Had he met my mom yet?"

"Very young, maybe not even through growing into a man, and no she wasn't with us. He met her here."

"Makes sense."

"I'm sorry you never got to meet her. Really nice

woman. She would've loved you dearly." The woman put her hand out and placed it on Tey's shoulder.

She felt tears welling up. Not for the grief of having lost someone, but for the grief of never having the pleasure to have met them. It was an odd feeling, and Tey wasn't sure how to place it. Like a loss of potential.

"I need to go," Tey said as she turned before the water started to run down her face.

"I understand. I'll be here if you ever want to talk. I have some stories about them I'd love to share with you."

Oh she has some stories alright. Stories you don't want to know. I can feel it. You want this lonely life so you don't have to go through loss ever again. Tey tried to ignore the voice in her head.

She went back to her room and sat on her bed. She watched the sand slowly trickle in through the imperfect seam of her window. It pooled on the floor in a mound. The little flecks were starting to tumble down the mound and create a larger base. She left the sand and laid back, her arms outstretched.

"I'm ready to go back to bed," she muttered. "Too emotionally draining of a day."

Tey turned her head and looked out the unbroken window. It wasn't even midday by her guesstimate of the sun's trajectory. "There's still so much to do," she said as her stomach growled. She sighed and stood back up. Heaving her backpack and grabbing her goggles, she made her way to the exit.

Outside the sand storm had died down. It still was not pleasant, she thought, as the sand smacked her face and made her eyes squint. She put the goggles on and wrapped a black bandana around her face.

The bazaar was finally starting to fill up with people and vendors. Some cleaned off their wooden tables, while others didn't and simply opened crates for people to look into.

It's a shame that it's all for nought. I am the reason for this. And I will be the end.

"What?" Tey asked as she turned her head every which way. No one paid her any mind. They had all lost enough daylight already, and no crazy person would stop them now.

You still don't get it, the voice said in her head.

"Who's there?"

It's just me. The reason the sand exists, the reason for all of this.

"You said that, but where are you?"

I'm in your head. Though, you've seen me already.

Tey felt herself make a face. Something similar to confusion or disgust. Like a stranger approaching her asking if she'd come home with him.

"Whatever," she said and walked further into the bazaar.

She looked around to see if there were any fruits or fresh vegetables someone was growing in their home. There wasn't. She assumed everyone packed quickly and made the best out of the daylight they had left.

Tey scanned the stalls and noticed regular vendors weren't there today. Probably from the sand storm, or everything they had was getting destroyed by the sand and they had lost their entire life's work just because they woke up this morning.

She sighed, pulled down her goggles and walked through the bazaar to the far-edge of the worn down city. This place had been forgotten by humanity, even God. The only thing she was sure of was that it had not been forgotten by the people who tried to survive here.

O Daughter Mine, your pain is my own. An outcast among your race. I am just like you.

"Who are you?"

We met in Gertrude's room. That small plant you saw. That is me. She's a nice woman. Come back and take me home. I'd love to meet you.

"That's not possible," she muttered as she kept walking. Her feet dragging through the sand. Tey no longer left footprints, just little divots as her legs shuffled along.

Your kind took me away from my home more than a century ago. I watched this place fall. I brought the sands for what they did.

"All of this is because of you?"

Take me and we will talk, O Outcast Mine.

Tey continued toward the edge of the city to look out on the hellscape of rolling dunes. "I must be getting delirious." But, then she felt drawn to the memory of that purple and green plant just sitting there. Like it was observing, taking in the world around itself.

The sun shifted and started to sink below the horizon. It cast long blue and gray shadows against the sand. The destroyed skyscrapers loomed and turned a metallic black. Tey felt a sense of comfort and disturbance all at once. Comfort for being outside without the winds whipping up the sand, like she was made to be outside with the sky above her. Disturbance for the ghastly images and shadows that surrounded her. *What were they hiding*, she wondered.

"Best get back," she whispered. A cool loneliness gripped her chest, and she wished she had someone in her life. Her parents, a partner, a relative. Anyone she could talk to and bond with. But none remained. The world, sickness, or the sand had taken them all. It was all too common for everyone around her, but they continued on all the same. She was the only one who felt stuck.

Tey lay in her bed, the dripping of sand through the seams had stopped. Tomorrow she would talk to Gertrude, ask her about the plant.

Goodnight, Tey.

She shut her eyes and dreamed a dreamless sleep. Her chest rising and falling to the emptiness of the world.

When Tey awoke, the sun had just started creeping back over the horizon as it finished its transit through the sky. She threw on her boots without smacking the sand out of them and walked to Gertrude's door. She knocked.

The old woman opened up.

"Nice to see you, Tey."

"You, too. I have a question, though."

"About your parents?"

"No," she said. "About that plant," she pointed into the room.

"Oh, this thing," she crossed the room, grabbed the potted plant and brought it back over.

"Has anything weird happened since you got it?"

Gertrude's eyes narrowed and her brows furrowed.

"No," she snapped.

"Where did your grandson find it? It's so different than anything we grow or have at the bazaar."

"I don't know exactly. Now leave!"

Tey was taken aback. Speechless. She didn't know what to say and walked down the hallway.

Hold on, the deep voice in her head returned.

Tey stopped, then looked back. Gertrude was shuffling over to her.

"I'm sorry, sweetie. I think you should take care of it."

"What?"

"You can take it, just let me see it when I want to." Gertrude put out her hands and handed the plant over to her.

"Okay," Tey said sullenly. She took the plant. "Weird," she muttered as the woman started to walk back to her room.

I told her she needed to give me away.

"Why?" Tey asked as she looked down.

Don't worry about it. Let's go back to your room.

Tey turned and walked to her room. She heard the woman start coughing up a lung. It was guttural and filled with mucous. She debated going back to check on her. The sand did that sometimes, created a sickness that made it hard to breathe. Gertrude's door slammed shut, and Tey decided against checking on her.

She placed the purple and green plant on her desk, then pulled up a chair and sat in front of it.

"Talk to me. Prove to me I'm not losing my mind."

Your name is Tey. Your parents are dead. You are alone on this planet as I am.

"Nothing new. Nothing I haven't said to myself

before." Tey felt a twang in her head. Like something was burrowing into her.

You wish you had never been born.

She sighed.

There are places east of here that have green trees and running water.

"Those are just rumors," she said. Tey knew she wasn't thinking these thoughts, that something really was talking to her now.

I know they're there. I created this place in the image of my home.

"What do you mean?"

The sands are my doing. This destruction is because of me.

Tey shook her head. That wasn't possible. One plant couldn't do all of this. Even if she had never seen the city before the fall, it wasn't possible.

There is so much you don't know. Worlds beyond the sky. Those stars you see twinkling, suns surrounded by planets. One was my home in your own solar system. But I drove your vehicle from the skies into this planet. Payback for taking me from my comfort.

"Vehicle? Solar system?" She was confused.

It doesn't matter. That knowledge is lost in time. I am not the first to be here, nor am I the last.

"There's more of you?"

Plenty. We all share the same mind, the same DNA. We

are all one, O Student Mine. I am not the one who drove that vehicle into your atmosphere, but I am all at once the same.

Tey's mind was swirling. There was so much information to take in, so much to try and put together from what this thing was telling her and what she had heard from the stories that were passed down.

"How long ago was this?"

Oh...I'd say close to two hundred years ago by now. At first, your kind tried to exterminate me, but that space station that fell from the sky did a lot to this region. It threw everyone into a panic worldwide. From there, it was all downhill, and I could turn this place into my own.

"So, you're a monster. An invader!" Her voice was filled with poison.

No. Your kind is the invader who took me from my home. You did this. This is all humanity's fault. I simply take what is now mine.

"If you did this, why can't we just live in peace?" Tey tried to diffuse the situation.

Impossible. I need an environment to live that is not compatible with human life. Though your kind is more resilient than I thought you'd be. Besides, I allowed you all to survive, you'd do the same thing you did in the past. I've learned that by studying you through the years. You find something that is different, then you obliterate it when you want. That's always your solution—killing.

"That's all you're doing in return!"

We aren't so different, but I value my life over yours.

Tey sighed, shook her head, then pulled open her closet doors. She strapped her metal and plastic armor on.

Where do you think you're going?

"Away from here. I need time to think."

You can't get rid of me, you know that. I've already spread throughout this place, you'll see. You all will see, O Student Mine.

"I'll think of a way to take care of it. Take care of this. To help these people I live around!"

You're a dreamer. I knew one of you before, O Dreamer Mine. His name was Ray.

"I don't care what his name was!"

He was like you. Always trying to fix things, but in the end, it was futile. He came to the same end they all did. And you will come to that end, along with everyone else after you until this place belongs to me and mine only.

Tey turned in a rage as she was about to leave her room. Her backpack caught her lamp with its small flame. It burst onto the floor as the glass surrounding it shattered. She heard the beast in her mind screech. Her eyes widened.

"So, you're scared of this?" she said as she bent down to pull the lamp off the floor, and stomp out the small fire that was there. There was no answer.

"Okay, then," she said as she opened a drawer, and

lit one of the precious matches she had as currency. She pulled a piece of rope out and hung it over the flame. The beast hissed. Tey crossed the room and held the burning rope on one of the purple leaves. The beast moaned, and Tey heard a door slam.

There was a banging, and Tey wondered who was outside of her room. She shook the flame off the rope and stomped it out on the floor. At the door was the old woman.

"Leave it alone!" she wailed.

"What?"

"I know you're hurting it! Leave my plant alone!" Gertrude screamed as she tried to push herself into the room.

"Get out!" Tey yelled back as she tried to keep the woman out.

"Help! Help! This girl's trying to hurt me!"

The hallway doors began to open up as Tey body-blocked the woman from entering.

"This woman's trying to come into my room! Someone help me. Please, just someone help me. I'm not hurting her."

Men and women began to gather and a few of them pulled the haggard woman away from Tey's room. Tey's heart was racing as they tried to restrain the woman.

Do you see what I can do? Do you see it? The devil I can place inside of you. You exist because I allow it.

"Just take her away," Tey said as she turned back to the plant and imagined lighting the entire thing on fire in a sick funeral procession on the sands.

"Leave it alone!" The woman wailed again.

Tey turned back and saw her eyes had turned all black, and blood began to coat her teeth. The men and women holding Gertrude struggled more and more. The woman turned and spit on one. His face contorted and his grip loosened. Tey watched him wipe away the blood with his hands. There was strands of black goo mixed with the blood, and the man emptied his stomach in front of them all.

"Get her out of here!" one of the other men yelled as he stopped trying to restrain the old woman and began to beat her.

It was lost now, Tey knew. The woman would be cast out of the community and probably killed along the way. Disagreements were fine, but assault was a different matter. Her life was forfeit for not adhering to the law.

You are barbarians for what will happen to her.

"Shut up," Tey whispered as she watched them drag the woman off, kicking and screaming. More than once she saw someone land a punch on her, but it didn't stop her fight, it only encouraged it.

Tey took a deep breath, looked at the plant, then

slammed her door shut as she walked opposite the way they dragged Gertrude off to.

Outside the air was arid. The sun felt like it was blistering her exposed skin. The cracks in her makeshift armor couldn't stop everything, no matter how hard she tried. Her blonde hair felt like it was dehydrating the farther she walked from her home.

In the shade of one of the old monoliths, she sat down and looked out, hoping to see life, to see green, but only brown sand looked back. She closed her eyes.

Let me show you something.

"I don't want to."

Open your eyes.

Tey listened though everything in her body told her not to. Before her stretched greens and blues. Plants, grass, and luminescent bugs flitting through the blades, which waved to her. There was a glowing aura coming off the vegetation that mesmerized her.

"What is this?" she asked as she gazed further and further to the horizon. In the distance she could see the monoliths she sat beneath. They were still broken and rusted against her new landscape.

This is what my world once looked like. This is what yours will be when I am done. Though you will not be here to see it.

"Then why are you showing me?"

Punishment. For what your kind took from me. I have

taken all from you, and I will see the beauty of this world one day when your bones are nothing but dust.

"No you won't. One day, someone will find a way to take you out!"

There was a hissing in her head, and Tey knew the plant was laughing at her. All around, the greens and blues started to shrivel up. The glowing from the plant life disappeared, and the bugs flying in front of her fell to the ground as they turned to dust, which blew away on whispers in the wind. Sand began to come in, and Tey pulled her goggles down over her eyes. She turned and began to run for home.

You'll never escape.

Tey knew there was only one thing she could do. She had burned it once, now she had to kill it. Rip it from its pot, and light it on fire. "It's the only thing I can do."

You won't get anywhere near me.

She ran as hard as she could toward the broken down buildings she grew up with. Her feet slapped against the sand around her. The bulk of her makeshift armor chaffed her skin. The wind picked up and the sand blew in harder than she had ever seen it. Tey pulled her bandana up over her mouth, and her pace slowed to a shuffle.

Look upon my work and despair. All around you, this wasteland is my own.

"You can't be doing this," she mumbled as she tried to shield any exposed skin to the stinging sand. She felt it ripping her hands and the warmness of blood beginning to trickle down her fingertips.

Watch as it stops.

As soon as the words finished, the sand storm died down, and Tey was once again able to see her home in the distance. She started to run again.

Uh-uh. Not so fast.

The sands picked back up again, and Tey wanted to scream as she was no longer able to see inches in front of her face. She put her hands out and shuffled forward, praying that she'd find a building to hide in. She bumped into a piece of metal.

Tey used her bleeding hands and felt for an opening. She knew she was at the edge of town, and there was a door somewhere close by. A metal protrusion gave way, and she tucked herself into an alcove. Her eyes adjusted a moment, and she was finally able to see the damage done to her arms. The skin was bright red, not only from the blood, but from the scraping of the sands against it. She turned to her left and looked for a nearby door. She found an entrance, and tucked herself into the building.

There was no one inside. Tey pulled her goggles off and removed her bandana before collapsing to the floor. Tears ran down her face, and she wished her dad was there with her.

"Why? Why me? Father, life has forgotten me."

The sun will die before your heart stops beating and your soul is brought peace.

Tey didn't reply. She sat in her squalor, surrounded by broken desks and chairs. She leaned her head back, and placed it on the cool wall behind her. It was a comfort for her as the pain in her hands began to well up.

"Why do you do this?"

Because of what your kind did to me centuries ago.

"But, *we* didn't do it to you. Our ancestors did.

And now I'm stuck on this hell because of them. I must turn this place into my home ever since I was kidnapped from the place I knew.

Tey sighed. There was no point arguing. She knew what revenge tasted like, and this *thing* clearly wanted revenge for the transgressions committed against it.

"I have to get home."

I have to get home. The voice in her head was mocking her now.

Tey cried harder. She only wanted to be left alone. To live her destroyed life as best she could. No drama, no pain, no hunger, no fucking sand. She just wanted to live. Exist in the world she was born into with as minimal stress as possible. But this plant clearly had other ideas. She hated it. Hated her ancestors. Hated the entire human race in this moment. The decisions of the past affected the future, her future, and for that, she wasn't so sure she could forgive them.

Now you understand me.

"We are nothing alike."

We are more alike than you think.

"No, we aren't," Tey exclaimed as she stood up, wiped her tears away, and pulled down her father's goggles. He wouldn't have wanted her to feel the hate in her heart. That wasn't how she was raised, she knew. She had to push on. Tey walked up a few flights of stairs and looked out onto the landscape.

The sand swirled and whipped through the broken building, but in the slight reprieves, she could see her home. She only needed to go outside, make a left, and stay in a straight line. *Easier said than done*, she thought to herself.

Tey stood at the same crack she had weaseled into. She took a deep breath, knowing that it would be the last without sand for a few minutes, and tucked herself back into the storm after pulling her bandana back up.

The sand stung her skin, and she put her hands in her pockets. It helped, but the holes in them still allowed for the brown crystals to find a way in. The garment grated against her already fragile skin. Tey gritted her teeth and put her head down. She could no longer see her feet as the storm picked up harder.

Tey shuffled, refusing to let her boots leave the ground. She hoped she was going in a straight line as her thoughts raced. This might be the place she died, out here on the sands, so close to home.

"When I get back, I'm burning it," she mumbled.

If you get back.

Tey tried to push the words from her head and couldn't decide if it were her inner monologue talking or the new found voice in her head.

The minutes seemed like hours, and Tey felt sand coming through new holes in her armor and clothing. It had started to whip so hard against her that the dirt and dust had created new pockets to tuck itself into. Even her boots felt like they offered little protection as she felt the sand pooling in between her toes. She looked up. The sky-rise wasn't far now.

Tey put her head back down and shuffled faster forward. Through her goggles, when the sand gave a little respite, she could see flashes of color. The bazaar flags were beneath her now, and she knew that the market had been decimated along with everyone's livelihood. She sighed and continued on until she bumped into the building.

Her hands felt for any opening they could find as her skin became more inflamed. She wished for gloves, but knew those were the hardest to come by. If she lived, she'd invest in them, no matter the price. She regretted the thought the second it came to her, but knew a few minutes of misery would be worth it. Her fingertips found a door, and she pulled as hard as she could against the piles of sand blocking her way.

The door moved just enough, and Tey squeezed through. Her armor catching the corners at times, so she needed to readjust. Everything stayed attached, and she fell to the floor with a thud. Quickly, she jumped up and pulled the door close to limit the amount of sand already beginning to pool inside.

The bandana was pulled from her face, her goggles lifted, and Tey began to shake the sand from her hair. It fell quickly from her scalp, and she was amazed how much continued to fall. She wanted a bath, but knew there was unfinished business.

I'll give it to you, O Warrior Mine. I didn't think you had it in you to brave the sands. My ancestors would have sang songs about you in the amphitheater. Behind all that glass, those worshippers of mine would have called you a god for ascending through the torment I would bring.

"I'm sure they loved you for it."

Feared. They feared my anger. Relished in my love.

Tey wanted to scream. This *thing* had done this before. Wherever it claimed to be from, whatever knowledge that was lost by her people was no use now.

She had a mission. Something her father had always prepared her for without her knowing. There was a determination now, one thing she needed to do. Save her people, no matter the cost.

Tey beelined it for the stairs, swung open a door, and plodded up to her room. There was no one around and she followed the square spirals up to the 8th floor. She swung the door open and ran for her room. As she turned a corner, she could see a mass of people standing in front of her door. Their eyes were black, with hints of purple in the center.

You cannot.

"I will," she said as she ran full force down the hallway and launched her shoulder into one of the men standing vacantly in front of her. He fell with a sickening thud as his head cracked against the white floor. Red began to pool underneath him.

Tey felt sick. "What have I done?" she said.

Just as the words came from her mouth, a man stumbled toward her and reached a slow hand out to grab her. She pulled back as his fingers leisurely tried to grasp her shirt. They were a disgusting black. Tendrils ran from his fingertips up his wrist and arm into his shirt. She looked up and saw the dead eyes, then down to see the tendrils ran from his leg to her bedroom.

"You're controlling them," she whispered.

O Genius Mine, nothing gets by you.

She picked her leg up and slammed her heel on one of the tendrils. The man in front of her opened his mouth and let out a guttural scream that shook Tey to her core. She couldn't describe the sound. It was inhuman, deep, and ricocheted through the hallway so hard that it almost made her eyes shake.

I have not felt pain like that in nearly a millennia. Thank you for reminding me what the forceful touch of a dead species feels like.

"You'll feel more than that," she stated emphatically.

The last time I let your kind touch me they probed me with needles. The last time I was abused, a warrior from my home tried to take my life.

"Then I am that warrior," she said as the man in front of her lurched again to grab her. Tey parried and knocked the man's head into the wall. He slumped to the floor, struggling to get up. His movements were janky and sporadic.

O Dreamer Mine, don't you see this is futile? I have survived everyone I have ever met. I am and will always be more than what you see. I am more than just one thing you see. We have sprouted throughout this land.

"There can't be more of you," she said as she ran closer to her room, swatting at the hands that tried to grab her.

There are more demons than you can imagine in hell.

Tey slammed herself into her door and broke it

from the frame. She slammed to the floor in a mass of splinters and sharp wood. Behind her, she could hear the sludging of feet as the husks of humans vied to follow her. Quickly she pushed herself off the floor and began opening her desk drawers to grab a match and anything that would burn quickly.

She held a notebook over the flame as three men with hollow eyes appeared in the doorway.

"Don't get any closer," she demanded. "I'll light this whole place up with us all inside."

You wouldn't.

No sooner than the words were heard in Tey's head, she placed the notebook into the flame and allowed it to light up. The husks moved closer, and she threw the notebook onto the plant. There was a screaming noise uttered from all the men...and the one in her head.

The plant caught fire, along with the old, dried out desk as embers fell from the burning paper. Tey ran forward into the mass of men blocking her escape. They did not budge as she threw herself into them. The black vines that twisted up their legs squeezed and forced their bodies to stack on each other. No amount of determination would get Tey through three full-grown men, and she knew it.

Tey backed up before they could grab her, and looked over to the plant. It was now fully aflame, along with her desk. The smoke rose, twisted to the ceiling and billowed out the door. She pulled her bandana up and her goggles down in the hopes it would stop some of the smoke from infiltrating her lungs.

"Just need a minute until it's dead, then they'll be free," she muttered as the human blockade pushed further into the room but still kept her only escape path blocked. Tey knew she was too high up to exit through a window. Her only way out was through, she knew.

You'll die in here with me, the voice in her head screeched.

As the men pulled forward, Tey tried to get an angle on them, hoping to sneak between whatever gap opened between their bodies. Each time she moved, the men moved to block her. The fire rose, along with the smoke, and Tey could feel the heat coming from her desk as the fire spread to the walls.

She ran, hoping to knock one of them down. Her boots clunked against the floor as she tried to get as much speed as possible, but it was useless. She clipped her own feet and fell flat on her face. The pain was immediate as her nose busted into the wood. Tey felt the bodies pile on top of her before she could get back up.

"No!" she wailed.

Yes.

Tey tried to move. She struggled as hard as she could, but the men on top of her weighed too much for her to get out from under. The smoke was becoming thick, and despite the bandana, Tey coughed from the soot and the burning in her lungs.

"Dad, I'm sorry. I couldn't save myself this time."

He'd be disappointed in you. The words trailed off as the fire became an inferno. All the garments and wood in Tey's room had now gone up in flames. She felt it spreading across the floor and blistering her hands.

It was the worst pain Tey had ever felt, and she only hoped that the end would come quick. She tried to breathe, but all she did was suck in smoke. Her head began to feel light, and shortly after Tey lost consciousness. The fire had taken up the room.

Her last thought was of her father. There was a smile on his face as he picked her up and carried her on his shoulders. In the last moments, Tey felt peace. She only hoped that killing the plant would afford some peace for whomever survived the spreading flame.

AN ILLUSION OF SOIL
WASHINGTON, 2339

You cannot stop what is inevitable.
"With the noose, or a knife, let me help you find hell."

ELIJAH WALKED UP to the log cabin covered in moss. The smell of copper, rotting flesh, and wet musky earth dominated his nostrils. He pulled the sleeve of his shirt into his palm and covered his mouth as he entered the old home.

He knew he'd have to shear another sheep and begin making a new shirt once he was finished here. As he looked down, he noticed the cuff was stained with pus and blood, neither of which were his own.

The foyer was dark, but from what he could see, nothing was out of place nor covered in the veins of infection. He nudged open another door in the cabin. A swarm of flies and parasitic bugs flew past his eyes. Elijah was glad his mouth was covered with his hand. He tried to swat them from his eyes as he walked inside the room.

The walls had been overtaken with the classic black veins that webbed their way from the source of the disease. His feet squished against the fleshy ground, creating the noise he hated most about doing his job. It felt like mud sucking at his boots as he walked.

He could live with the smell, almost became used to it at this point. Once he got working, he hardly noticed it, but the dreadful escape of fluid from the small pustules below his feet made him wish he were deaf.

Elijah traced the lines of the infection through the room and followed them into the kitchen from the far side door. Next to a the cast iron stove it sat, waiting. Waiting to talk. Waiting to be awakened and learn of Elijah and its fellow brothers and sisters.

"This one likes warmth," Elijah mumbled to himself. His voice gruff, almost hoarse from the stagnant air in the cabin.

Nice to meet you, Elijah.

He pulled his knife out and an old piece of flint.

Don't do that. We're just getting started.

"No talking, I've been through this before."

There was silence, a moment frozen in time until

Elijah felt his eyes wince. He knew the infection was probing his memories.

I see this. How unfortunate that they all died at your hands. An anomaly? You? A step in evolution to be unbothered by us? Ahhhh. How peculiar and unfortunate. I only wished to be warm in this room.

"Then you will be warm," Elijah replied as he walked to the cabinets searching for anything that would make good kindling.

He found a wooden bowl, aged, and dried out.

"This will have to do," he said as he pulled his knife and started to cut the bowl into thin strips. The light brown color contrasted against the dark table as he piled the shavings.

Why do that? We could have so much fun. Such great memories were once made in this house.

"Your kind does not work on me."

There was silence as Elijah continued to dismantle the bowl.

How? The voice asked.

"Don't know," he grumbled as the sound of his knife against the bowl filled the room.

That's impossible.

"Never worked. Your kind cannot access my mind. Only speak to it."

That's impossible! It shrieked.

Satisfied with the kindling, Elijah placed the withered bowl next to his neat pile, and pulled the piece of flint back out from his pocket. He stroked his knife against it until a small spark landed in the light brown mass. He leaned in, clasped his hands around it, noticing the softness against his calloused skin, and blew until the smoke billowed around him.

Elijah watched as he placed the small fire back onto the table. He walked to the cabinets and kicked them from their hinges so he could break them into smaller pieces. Food for the flame that would raze the house.

You're a monster.

"I am only what your kind did to us. I wish to be the nightmare that keeps all of you up at night."

The flies had started to disperse as Elijah laid small strips of worn wood onto the flame. They crackled as the fire easily caught and became larger.

You are what we have always searched for. An enigma to us. The thing only spoken of in solitude. The one who we can not control.

"I am the demon sent from Hell to drag you back." Elijah's voice was gruff beneath his gray beard, which muddled the words.

He stepped back to watch as the fire started to spread along the long, thin pieces of wood and down onto the table. He heard the sickness from the pustule sac sigh as it released spores into the air.

"That won't work. I figured that out a long time ago. Your children will suffocate just as you will."

There was no reply. Elijah knew the truth, and the sickness did too. It was only a matter of time until it passed on to whatever afterlife it would dwell in.

Elijah watched the fire engulf the table and start to whip into the air as the smoke turned black. He turned and left the kitchen to wait outside.

The day was still young and his job was complete. He'd return back to town, maybe grab a bowl of gruel, or a woman to sit in his lap. Either way, he felt a sense of lonesome accomplishment. It was boring work for him now, but he knew it had to be done. The existence of everyone relied on him.

The flames whipped out of the windows, and the small wooden cabin was lit up.

"This one might spread to the trees, but it's collateral damage at this point."

He walked away through the woods, back toward town, back to let them know to keep buckets of water ready—just in case. It's the least they could do.

The sheriff greeted him as he approached.

"Is it done?" he asked.

"Yes. The fire might spread, but it is done."

"I'll let them know. And here," he extended his hand, "for your work."

Elijah put his hand out and was fed seven silver

coins and four copper ones. They were stamped with old people from the Before-Time.

"Seems a little light this time," he gruffed.

"We haven't had many visitors. But I received a letter from a nearby town that they're having infestation problems. They asked for your services," the sheriff said as he produced a letter with a black seal on it.

"Thank you," Elijah said as he grabbed it and unfolded the paper inside. He quickly scanned the contents. "Ten? That's borderline desolation. How are they still going?"

"Just barely. They've lost fifty people in the last three months. A third of their population. Their coffers should be full from the wealth they acquired from the deaths."

"I'll head out tomorrow," he handed one silver coin back to the sheriff. "Have a horse ready for me with water and dried meat."

"Of course, Elijah," he bowed.

Elijah nodded and walked into town. The old saloon on the right, the post office on the left. He heard of the old cities some people still dwelt in made of metal, but he had never been. One day his abilities might be welcome there, but for now, he had to protect this new settlement he had been welcomed in.

The saloon was mostly empty, only a couple stragglers who were trying to escape their husbands or wives could be seen sitting at the bar. No one resided at any of the tables near the entrance. Elijah closed the wooden door behind him before he took off his coat and placed it on one of the knobs along the wall. It drooped down lower than the rest, which kept it company.

"What're ya havin'?" a gruff voice resounded from behind the bar as Elijah's chair scraped across the floor.

"The usual," he replied, as he laid his hands against the smooth top of the bar.

The bartender placed a small glass in front of him and filled it with a brown liquid. Elijah graciously picked it up and took a sip. It burned and filled his nostrils.

"New batch, Alex?"

"Sure is. Been runnin' low on things, had to use more corn this time around."

"I don't dislike it."

"Me either, but it ain't my best work."

Elijah nodded and looked around at the men and women sitting near him. They knew him, but few talked to him. He figured it was because of fear that somehow he might be infected by the plants. But they knew, even if he touched one, or breathed in its spores, nothing happened. It never did.

"How did today go?" Alex asked.

"Same as it always goes. That sickness is gone from the house, but the house no longer remains."

"Were they alive still?"

"No. Pustules and flies everywhere. It had taken them over and fed on them. I expected it to be honest. We found them too late. I keep telling the sheriff we need to keep track of everyone coming in for supplies every few days. If we don't hear from anyone within a week, we have to check on them."

"Damn shame," Alex shook his head.

"It's a shame no one thought anything of it until no one had seen them for a month. Who knows how long they had it, or where they got it from. I might have been able to find who brought it in."

Alex grunted in agreement.

Elijah looked down to his glass and chugged the rest in remembrance for the family the town lost.

"Another?"

"Yes, and whoever is available." Elijah reached in his pants pocket and pulled a silver coin.

"Marge is upstairs, second door on the left."

"The brunette?"

"Ay, that's the one."

"I liked talking to her last time."

"She's a good one," Alex said as he poured Elijah another drink.

He reached to the glass, which had slight fingerprints on it and walked it up to the room with him.

Elijah stepped through the door and kicked it

closed behind him. Marge was sitting on the bed, staring at him. Her brown eyes were soft, and her cheekbones had grown tighter since the first time they met.

"Nice to see you again," Elijah said.

"You too, darlin'."

Elijah crossed the room and placed his drink on the bedside table. He sat down and undid the laces of his boots. His feet stunk like vinegar. His shirt and pants didn't smell much better.

"I'm going to draw myself a bath," he said.

"Water is already hot, just pour it in."

He nodded, grabbed his clothes from the floor, and walked to the bathroom. He placed everything in a small metal sink and dumped water on top of them to soak. The water steamed and turned between a mixture of brown and red. He filled the tub with what was left and sat down in it.

"Here's some soap," Marge said as she came into the bathroom, her body naked like his.

"Thank you," he said as he reached out and grabbed the small bar made from animal fat. It was soft in his hand, almost too soft with consideration for his calluses. Like it wasn't even there. If it had any less weight to it, Elijah would have sworn that his eyes were playing a trick on him and that he wasn't touching anything at all.

"Would you mind if I had this moment to myself?" Elijah looked up to Marge's doe eyes.

She nodded and walked out of the bathroom, closing the door behind her.

Elijah lathered his body, feeling the soap sting small cuts on his forearms. The white foam quickly turned brown the moment it touched his skin, and more than once he found himself scrubbing his arms and legs under the water before lathering up again.

The hair on his body had grown coarse from the work. His skin thick from the manual labor he did tending to his small home and the fires he continued to burn throughout the nearby towns. Even now, as he sat in the warm water, it didn't feel like much against his desensitized skin.

He breathed deep and smelled the burnt wood still on his body, along with the all-too-familiar stench of pustules. It reminded him of old eggs as it lingered under the smell of smoke. Few, he was sure, knew the smell, and probably attributed it to simply how he was. But he knew all too well, the only ones who knew the stench were the ones who died from the plants as they were enveloped in their homes.

Elijah sighed as he rinsed the last bit of soap from his body and groaned as he stood up. Sitting too long always made his muscles tighten, and his legs felt like anchors beneath him.

He grabbed a cloth and dried himself. Before leaving the bathroom, he pulled a small plug from drain of the tub and hung it over the edge. Elijah didn't have to do it, as the cost of the room covered the cleanup, but he felt he should at least make someone's life a little bit easier. After all, that was his job. Make the lives of everyone in the town easier, and keep their minds slightly more at ease.

The bathroom door opened before him, and Elijah stepped through to grab his glass of whiskey. He lay on the bed as he watched Marge move across the room. Her skin was taught against her body. She wasn't bad to look at. Her breasts were small. He figured he could hold both of them in one hand if it were possible. There was little hair on her besides that on her head. She was soft, untainted by the world outside of this place. He watched her cross the space between and lay on her side next to him.

"How was today?"

"Not good," he said as he pulled another sip of whiskey from the glass.

"I'm sorry that you're cursed to be the one to take care of this."

"Me too," he replied. "But it's a curse I don't take for granted. It's my Godly duty."

"Did you see anyone there or was it too late?"

He shook his head. "I didn't go looking for anyone. Just took care of the mess and turned the place to ash."

"Why? Why not look?" Her eyes held sadness as she asked.

"I can tell by the smell and the flies. Once they start coming around, there's nothing left. Just decaying bodies with small vines coming from them leading to the larger sac and the plant itself. I can't do anything to save them once they've gotten to that point."

"It's always at that point when you get there, isn't it?"

He grunted in affirmation. "Always is. No need to go and see how much is left of their faces when I get there. I'm not sure there's any way to save them, really. I've only caught one early enough to have any recognizable features. But still, I had to burn them all."

"What was that like?" she asked.

"I could still see them—all their features. The way their eyes had sunken in and hadn't turned to decay yet. Their teeth were still grimacing in pain as the vines dug into their skin. The clothes they wore were still fresh, almost clean underneath the plant life growing over them. But when I spoke to them, nothing came out. It told me they could hear me, that they wanted to talk, but it controlled them. It controlled their movements and kept them alive to feed off of them. It's something I wouldn't wish on anyone else. To have to deal with that, to see it up close. I'd rather keep it away from everyone in every town if I can. To never have to suffer the way those people suffer. That's my goal. My mission. To save this planet, to find a way to bring back the society we all hear about in stories. Before the plants and the sand swept it all away."

Elijah looked over to Marge. Her eyes were softer, almost wet. He rolled over and put his arm around her, feeling the curve of her hip.

"I'm used to it now," he said.

"I hope you mean it and aren't just saying that," she replied before kissing him.

***

Elijah got dressed and wandered downstairs. He left Marge sleeping. He took once last look at the bed before closing the door. She was wrapped in the blankets and had all the pillows surrounding herself.

"She's a good one," he muttered to himself as he pulled the door quietly shut. He wanted to smile and daydream of another life where, just maybe, they could have been together, but there was no use.

His boots clunked on the stairs down to the bar. He placed his empty whiskey glass on the edge.

"Sheriff's got yer horse waitin' down by the gate," the gruff bartender's voice boomed.

Elijah nodded and walked toward the door to collect his jacket.

"Ya be needin' anythin' 'fore you set off?"

Elijah paused and fumbled in his pocket for another silver coin.

"Pass me a bottle," he said as he walked back to the bar and placed the coin down.

"Ay. That's what I were thinkin' too," the bartender smiled a toothy smile and handed Elijah a bottle filled with brown liquid.

He put his hand on it before being interrupted.

"You take care of yerself now, ya hear? I want you back in this town."

"Always do," Elijah replied and took the bottle outside with him.

The sun was up again, and the sky was the bluest he had seen in a while. There was no cloud coverage, but the air was cool for mid-Spring. He walked through town and, as he did, he watched all the men and women who had wandered from their homes to gaze upon him as he strode down the road to get his horse.

"Nice seeing you, Elijah," the sheriff greeted him by tipping his hat.

"You too," he said as he walked by and stuffed the bottle of liquor into the pack atop the horse.

"Five days worth of food and water on 'em. Days

ride out, days ride back, and a couple in there just in case."

"Thanks," he said as he mounted the horse.

"Listen," the sheriff said, as he closed the distance between them and looked Elijah in the eyes. "If this place ain't worth saving, then burn it all. Their letter was dire, so I don't know how many are left or where they'll be. Check the Post and general store. That's my best guess."

"No. They'll be spread out if the infection is that bad. Wouldn't risk coming all together and dying in one spot. Saloon'll be closed too. No reason to be fuckin' and drinkin' with strangers."

"Ay, I hear ya. You know better than me with these things."

"Ay," Elijah replied.

"Come back safe, Elijah," the sheriff said as he stepped away from the horse.

He nodded and kicked his heels into the horse after taking the reins. It trodded on the road out of town and into the woods. The silence engulfed them, with only the clopping of hooves as company as they went.

***

Elijah set up camp about halfway to town. From the

pack, he pulled a blue tarp and strung it over a line he tied around two trees.

"Best not start a fire tonight," he mumbled to himself.

The weather was warm enough with his clothes, and he didn't want to draw any attention from anyone who might also be out on the trail, though he knew it was less than unlikely these days. The infections were growing worse, and he was working more. After he set up his small shelter, he unrolled a blanket for the ground and poured water into a dish for the horse, which drank thankfully.

"They packed you some carrots, too," he said as he scavenged through the supplies the sheriff took the liberty in packing for him.

Elijah fed the horse then tied it to the tree before feeding himself salted pork from a glass jar. It wasn't his favorite, he'd admit to anyone, but it did the job of satisfying the grumble in his stomach.

The stars above were out on the clear night, and he took a moment to appreciate them through the canopy.

"At least I can enjoy this moment whenever I'd like," he breathed deeply before standing up and putting himself to bed.

***

The morning sun creeped through the trees and crested upon his head. He woke to its warmth, and quickly packed up camp while his companion drank again. Then he left in haste, hoping that maybe, just maybe, there was something or someone able to be saved in the town.

The clopping of hooves continued on until he saw the distinct entrance to the town. Two massive pieces of lumber with another stretched between the two. And just beyond, a few buildings to gather, partake, and live were stretched out on two sides of a dirt road.

No one greeted him as he came into the town. No sheriff, no bartender, no prostitute, not even a simple farmer. The sound of emptiness lingered as he hopped off and led his horse to a hitching post. He tied a loose knot and walked to the Saloon, even though his sheriff told him no one would be there.

Elijah knocked on the wooden door, and as his fist hit it, the door creaked open. There was no warm body to greet him, no ruckus that he was interrupting. He turned and left the door open. The general store was the same, though this time, the door was locked. Lastly, Elijah tried the sheriff's door.

"Who's there?" a voice asked after the quick bang, bang, bang, of his hand.

"I've been sent to help," Elijah replied.

"You the burner?"

"If that's what you call me over here, yeah." He stepped back and waited from the door to open.

The door opened slightly, and a man who couldn't have been older than his mid-twenties stood at the door.

"How do I know you ain't infected, too?"

"My reputation should stand up to that."

"Yeah, I guess."

"Where is everyone?" Elijah asked.

"There ain't many left. Post comes through sometimes. But after that letter, no one come by this place no more."

"Where's the sheriff?"

"Same as everyone else, dead or staying away from each other."

"How'd you get in there then?"

"He left it open, and I locked him out."

"Why would you do that?"

"Better to save myself. That sheriff ain't right. He been stealing and hiding supplies here to save hisself."

"You got anyone in there with you?" Elijah tried to peer over the man's shoulder, but the room behind him was dark.

"My younger sister. Our parents went to check on some neighbors and never came back."

Elijah nodded.

"What other places might have someone still around to speak with?"

"The Browns should be at the end of the road on the left hand side," the man made a motion with his head.

"And where do I go for the pestilence?"

"I don't know that word."

"The plants."

"The Saloon got hit last, from what I heard. Every building on that side of the street's been empty. It could be in all of them. Then if you go past the Browns, there are a few farms. All of them got hit, I think."

"So, just you, your sister, and the Browns are left?"

"As far as I know."

Elijah sighed. "Your note said a third of the town was lost. It's been more than that."

"Since I sent it, yeah. Everyone's been taken except us."

"When's the last time you saw the Browns?"

"Yesterday. We step out onto the road and wave to make sure someone's still left. I gotta check when the sun is highest in the sky."

"I see," Elijah replied and turned away.

"Whatcha gonna do?"

"Look through the Saloon and make my way down to the Browns to talk."

"Help yourself to anything in there."

"I planned on it."

"Wait," the man said as he opened the door more and thought about stepping out. "Can I come with you back to town when you're done?"

"How many days supplies do you have?" Elijah asked.

The man looked puzzled a moment.

"How many days?" he asked again.

"About 10 if we don't start eating less."

"Let me do my job, and if you aren't infected when I'm done here, I'll ride out and ask. Then I'll come back with what my Sheriff says."

"Okay," the man looked dejected.

"I'm sorry," Elijah said as he observed the man's face. "I can't risk bringing someone into town who might be infected without knowing it."

"How long 'til you know if I ain't or not?"

"There's no specific way, but if I burn through everything here in the next two days, ride back, and come back here and you're still looking like you do today, then I think you're okay. Usually takes hold of someone within a day or so. Sometimes faster. Never seen it take longer than two days, though."

"I understand. Must've taken my parents faster, then."

"I'm sorry for your loss. Close the door and stay in. I'll let the Browns know you're still alive."

"Thank you."

Elijah nodded his head and made his way back to his horse and the Saloon.

He grabbed the reins to the horse and led it back across the dirt road. The dried leather strained as he tied it to a post outside an unmarked building. Elijah crossed back and opened the door to the Saloon. Inside the area was musty, but didn't smell of the death he had grown accustomed to. It simply seemed vacant and filled with the smell of alcohol and sex.

Upstairs there was a lingering smell. He followed his nose to the last door and opened it. Inside lay bodies, not decaying with pustules and infestation, simply a sad death. A man and a woman were intertwined, each with blood and chunks of flesh splattered against the wall behind them.

"Suicide," he muttered in sadness to himself. "Can't say I blame them. Better to go out on your own terms if you think you're infected, than to die a slow and painful death by those damned things."

Elijah quietly closed the door and didn't scavenge the room for any supplies. He knew better. It was a disgrace to disturb the peace of a suicide. The unwritten code all towns agreed to. Leave their possessions behind so they can collect them in the afterlife.

His boots clunked down the steps. Before leaving, he grabbed a few bottles of alcohol, one of which he poured across the floor to the door. He reached into his pocket and produced a box of matches, lighting one. Elijah knelt to the ground and let the alcohol catch. He left to pack the bottles onto his horse.

"What'd you do that fer?" the man appeared and asked Elijah from behind his door.

"What's your name, kid?"

"Aurion."

"'Aurion,' got it. That place was a suicide. Better to let them burn in peace. Besides, it's not connected to any of the other buildings. Wind's not blowin', just gotta take care of business right now," Elijah said as he turned and walked down the road toward the Browns. He didn't have time to continue this conversation. Too much work to do, too little time to stand around yapping with a stranger

As he walked, Elijah looked around for any sign of life. He expected that maybe a straggler would come see the fire, wondering what the smell was, but no one appeared, not even the Browns.

Their house was modest, as most seemed to be. A single window looked out to the street. Elijah walked up to the door, banged a couple of times, and stepped back to wait for a response. There was none. He approached and did it again. No response.

"Christ," he sighed and stepped over to the window to peer inside. Nothing looked out of the ordinary, and there was no smell emanating from the residence.

He looked up to the sun, "probably another hour or so, then they'll come out to check on Aurion," he muttered before crossing the street to sit in the shade of a building.

Elijah produced himself a rolled cigarette, one of the few he still had, and lit it. The smoke swirled nicely into the air in front of him. He enjoyed the smell of the tobacco, the sweetness and muskiness. It helped cut through the death that clung to his clothes.

The sun crested the noon sky, and the door across the street opened to a man and woman. Their white clothes were stained with red mud and yellow blotches, Elijah noticed. He flicked the ash off of his cigarette and put it in his pocket. He stood up and raised his hand.

"I'm from the next town over," he announced. "I tried knocking but no one answered."

"We were downstairs," the man replied but did not step from outside the doorway.

"I'll be taking care of the infection around here. Just wanted to see how you were feeling."

"Fine," the man replied but still chose not to step outside.

"Aurion's doing good too. He told me about your schedule. What were you doing downstairs?"

"Canning," the man was curt.

"Can I get your first name?"

"Riley."

Elijah let a pause hang in the air.

"And your wife's?"

"None of your concern."

"Okay then." Elijah didn't feel as welcomed by these people as he would have hoped. "I'll be taking care of the plants in the area. Feel free to talk to me if I'm in the area, but don't follow me if you want to stay alive." He turned and walked back to Aurion's new home.

"How do we know you're not infected? Or a pawn for those things," Elijah heard the man shout as he was halfway back to his horse.

Elijah sighed and turned, "My reputation speaks for itself, or I wouldn't be here. Now, let me work." He turned back away from the man and continued working. There was a question asked, but Elijah didn't bother to listen to what it was.

"You see them?" Aurion asked as Elijah shuffled through his belongings.

"Yep. Not too friendly."

"They were always a closed-off family."

"Fine by me. I'll be working now," he said as he walked away to the homes across the street. To his left the Saloon was now in a full inferno. The smoke whipped black against the sky and the wood cracked.

As he approached a string of houses, he smelled the pestilence inside.

"This is a big one," he muttered to himself.

The wooden door was barred shut as he tried to open the first house. He braced himself against the door and slammed his shoulder into it. There was a groan and creak. Elijah repeated the process two more times before the latch gave way. He barreled inside and almost lost his footing. There was a new pain in his shoulder, and he knew it would be days before it went away.

Flies buzzed throughout the home and swept themselves out into the open air. He grabbed a black handkerchief from his back pocket and covered his mouth so nothing had the chance of flying into it.

Ahhh, a new morsel to feed on.

Elijah smiled beneath the handkerchief as he walked through the living room and into the kitchen. Nothing. Not a single strand on the floor, but the smell was overpowering.

"Biggest one yet," he mumbled.

I heard you.

"I'm glad," he announced louder.

Who are you?

"I'm Death, and I've come to collect."

I am also Death. And I have collected.

"Not in the way that I do," Elijah said as he opened a door. It was a bedroom. Inside there were four sacks of what used to be people. The brown pustules had taken over, and green vines webbed away from them. Against a far wall was the plant he was looking for. Green with purple flowers growing larger from the nutrients it was collecting.

You know what you've lost by coming here.

"Not what you think. Go ahead, look deeper."

Elijah felt a small twinge in his head where the voice resided, but nothing happened.

I don't understand.

"Your kind never does when I come knocking."

How peculiar. An evolutionary misstep in humanity. So be it. You'll end the same. You all end the same. For hundreds of years now.

"I've heard the story," Elijah cut the plant off. "Taken from your home, traveling the stars because of my ancestors, only to crash here on Earth and demand payment for what we did to your kind. The thing is," Elijah said as he produced his flint and knife, "even though you can harass us, you can't communicate far and wide to all your brothers and sisters I've taken the lives of."

Who are you?

"Like I said, I am Death. The demon that should haunt the dreams of your kind. I've come to demand payment for what you did to this town." Elijah struck the flint above the bed. Sparks spread onto the sheets, and they took almost immediately. He did it a few more times as the plant released its spores. It was futile. The smoke was beginning to rise, and soon it would engulf the entire block.

Elijah walked out before the plant tried to continue the conversation with him. The only thing he heard as he closed the front door behind him was the distinct shrieking it created, like claws on metal.

He rubbed his fingers across his face and down his cheeks as he walked back to his horse and opened a bottle of liquor he recently stole.

"Done already?" Aurion's voice appeared.

"No. Just getting started," he said as he took a swig from the bottle and put the cork back in.

"That bad?"

"Always bad, if it's one person or an entire family, it's always bad. Be grateful you don't have to see it."

"But I'm also not immune, so for that I am ungrateful."

"A blessing and a curse, that's what this all is."

Elijah watched Aurion nod as he closed the door.

"Something ain't right with that kid," he mumbled to himself. Before dwelling too long on it, Elijah made his way down the dirt road, past the Browns' and toward the farms just beyond the town.

"Maybe some of their crops will still be good. It is harvesting season after all."

The first two farms went up in flames quickly. Elijah

stepped inside each one, found the infestation, and burned them without conversation.

The third farm was farther out, and he reckoned it was newer by the luster of the wood it was built from. There weren't years of weather tied to it yet.

He stepped inside and the smell of infection lingered, but it wasn't prominent.

"This one is fresh," he said as he walked up the stairs toward the bedrooms.

A visitor.

"I don't have time for this," he announced as he opened the door.

But we've only just met.

"And it will be the last time," Elijah pulled his flint out and scanned the room. His heart sank. In the corner a man and a woman's body lay propped against the wall. Their features were still there and he could even see the whites of their eyes.

"Goddamnit," he muttered.

Would you like to join them? They can still hear you.

"You'll pay, you'll all pay." A sense of guilt washed over him. If only he had gotten the note a few days sooner, these people might have had a chance. A chance at life, a chance to grow and be a part of the safety he provided for his small town. He lit the fire and let the guilt wash over him.

"It's done," Elijah said as he returned to Aurion. The

sun had mostly set, and the sky was alive with fire and soot.

"Thank you," he replied.

"I'll be back." Elijah walked to his horse and went to mount it.

"Not staying the night?"

"No," he replied with no further explanation. He knew that he was emotionally drained from not being able to save the family. Maybe, just maybe, he'd come back and be able to save Aurion, though his gut told him otherwise.

"I'll see you in a few days then," Aurion said before closing the door.

Elijah nodded and made his way out of town and back home.

The stars were out, he noticed, as he got further away from the smoke trying to block the sky. They were like the eyes of old gods keeping a watch on the world below, but doing nothing to save humanity. That was his job, Elijah knew. He was meant to save what little was left of them, or at least protect them as best he could. What was the difference anyway? After him, who would take on his job? He fathered no kids, so he had no chance of passing his immunity on. He breathed a long breath and chose to keep riding throughout the night rather than stop and rest. He doubted sleep would come easy tonight anyway.

The horse walked until the sun came up again, and once it reached its peak, Elijah was able to see the wooden posts informing him that home wasn't far away.

"Almost there," he whispered into the horse's ear and patted it on the neck. "Then you can get some rest."

He hitched the leather straps to a post and grabbed his pack along with all his supplies before he made his way to see the sheriff. The door groaned as he pushed on it.

"Back so soon?" the sheriff looked surprised to see him.

"Yeah," his voice raspy.

"Any luck?"

"One guy and his sister, who I never met, and a family who wouldn't come out."

"Not entirely unusual."

"The one kid asked to come with his sister."

"What'd you tell 'em?"

"I'd speak to you first and wait a few days before heading back to see if any infection took hold."

"We don't really need any more hands here, but I'm sure they could be of use on one of the farms. Any animals left over there?"

"None that I saw at the farms. Food looked decent enough if it survives the fires. Might be able to get some seeds from the plants and start a new plot around here."

"We have a few open houses just beyond yours."

"I recall."

"If he's not infected, you can bring him. If he is, just grab what supplies you can."

"And the family?"

"If they ain't ones for talkin', they ain't ones for workin' with us."

Elijah knew what that meant. They'd be left to their own devices, even if they ran out of food, trading was no longer on the table. It was a hard truth, but he understood why it was there. Why help people who didn't want to accept your offer to be a part of the community? If they felt they could handle it by themselves, well, the sheriff believed they damn well should handle it by themselves. It kept their community tight knit, that's for sure, and it protected what little the town had from anyone who thought they might be able to infiltrate and leave whenever they felt like it.

"I know what you're thinking," the sheriff said.

"I always think it, but it's for the best. We have too much good going here to risk any of it."

The sheriff nodded. "Get some rest, take whatever you want from that town you'd like to keep for yourself as payment. Just bring me back some seeds."

"Anything you want me to keep any eye for?"

"Maybe some alcohol or any animals that might be roaming around. A pig roast would do nicely for the morale of the town. Just use your judgment. I'll have an extra horse for you along with some empty satchels for supplies. When do you plan on leaving?"

"Day after next. Give him some time."

"You trust him?"

Elijah made a face. "Not entirely. Didn't meet his sister."

"I'll make sure you have a gun then."

Elijah blinked. Bullets were worth a house or two to anyone who was willing to trade them. He heard of places that could still forge them, but rarely did any travelers come through bringing them. In fact, the last time they had someone who claimed they were from the town that traded them was almost two years ago.

"Thank you," he said.

"Still remember how to use it?"

"Sure do, not the best shot with it, but I can handle myself."

"Just don't keep it fully loaded in case he makes a move for it."

Elijah nodded.

"Now go get some rest. I can tell you've been up all night."

"Will do," Elijah said as he turned away to head home.

"And Elijah? Stay safe, okay? You're the only one keeping this place together, and you know that deep down, I'm just here to be the figurehead. These people care more about you than they do their spouses and kids."

Elijah sighed. He knew it was true, but he didn't want the glory or admiration. He just wanted to live his life.

Elijah's home felt cold as he stepped inside. Part of him wanted a family to run up and greet him whenever he got home, but the other half worried that he might be covered in spores that would end up killing them. He walked upstairs to his room and took off his boots at the door. The dried mud left stains on the floor.

As a creature of habit, Elijah saw the dust collecting around the room except where he lay his knife and flint. On the end table, there was a perfect outline of each. He didn't take off his clothes as he laid on top of the sheets, closing his eyes.

The sun peaked through the window, waking him.

"Has it been a whole day already?" he whispered to himself just before his hands rubbed the crust from his eyes.

Elijah shuffled to the bathroom. The water bucket on the floor was still full. He reached inside and grabbed the rag from it. He wiped down his arms and face, then threw it back in the bucket.

Outside, the town was bustling. He walked across the street and grabbed the two horses attached to each other. His muddied boots were placed into the straps, and he rode away from the town he called home, and he made his way for the town everyone called danger.

The sun had risen again by the time Elijah got to the town. All that was left were smoldering buildings and the stench of burnt wood. He got down off his horse and hooked it to a post across from where Aurion had shacked up. His knuckles rapped against the door and Elijah stepped away waiting for Aurion.

The seconds turned to minutes before there was an answer, but Aurion opened the door and didn't have a sickly look to him, simply a tired one.

"You're back," he said.

"And you're still alive."

"I am."

"How's your sister?"

"Good. Are we coming back with you?"

"Yes."

"Would you like to come inside and meet her while we get our things together?" Aurion asked.

"Sure," Elijah replied. It couldn't hurt, he thought to himself.

He walked up to the door and followed Aurion through the Sheriff's building to the back room that usually housed any criminals. The place smelled rank, like a mix of body odor and something he couldn't quite place.

"Denny, say 'hi' to Elijah. He's the man I've been

telling you about, the one who's going to take us from here." Elijah followed Aurion's voice.

He stepped through the door frame and saw the back of a woman's head. It was covered in strands of infection. The purple hue was all too familiar. He stepped back and put his hand to his knife.

"You're immune, too," Elijah stated.

"Immune? What do you mean?" Aurion looked up from his dead sister and locked eyes with Elijah.

He brought me another subject, the voice of the plant erupted in Elijah's head. *Thank you for coming to feed me.*

"Of course, Denny. Gotta keep your energy up before we make the trip out of here."

"You've lost it," Elijah said. "Goddamnit," he muttered to himself. There was hope for once, and just like that, it was gone. But how? How is this man immune too? It didn't matter. If he were mistaking a plant for his real sister, there was no saving him. His mind was gone, even if his body wasn't.

"What do you mean that I've lost it?" Aurion looked back at Elijah.

"She's dead! Can't you see that? She's just fucking dead. The plant is talking to you."

"Elijah, you're talking nonsense. Are you okay?" Aurion started approaching him with his hands up.

"Don't fucking come closer," Elijah shouted as he pulled the revolver from the back of his waistband and aimed it at Aurion's heart. There was a sadistic look that came across Aurion's face, something that made even Elijah tremble.

"Oh, we've been waiting for you," Aurion said, but his voice was different, other worldly. "Waiting for the day the man who cannot be stopped came into town."

"No," Elijah said. "That's not possible."

"It is, my friend."

And it always will be.

"We were finally able to evolve in a way that let us take over your bodies."

It just took a little time to get things working right.

Both voices answered simultaneously in his head and through Aurion's mouth.

"Then you know how this ends," Elijah said as he pulled the trigger and shot through Aurion's chest three times.

I didn't think you'd have the guts to kill one of your own.

"You don't know what I'd do to keep humanity alive," he chimed back as he holstered his weapon and pulled his flint and knife. He struck it.

No! The beast shouted as it released spores into the air.

"I will never hesitate to end any of you or any one who threatens my species," Elijah spit.

The small flares from the flint were smoldering on the

floor as he ran back to the entrance looking for paper. He found some in the desk and struck his flint again, making sure that this place would go up as quickly as possible.

Elijah left the conflagration behind and headed for home.

As the day turned to night, he began to question himself.

"How could they have done this? Was Aurion immune? Hanging around his sister for so long, he must have been. Those things can't control what they release...can they?"

His mind began to spin and his stomach turn. It was the worst of people that he saw. Always the worst. The only best he got was a "thank you" and to be shunned from the people he struggled to protect at any given moment.

Elijah kicked his heels into his horse.

"Might as well make good time so I can sleep in my own bed. Take a day off. Something. Anything. Just let me suffer alone with myself for a moment," he muttered.

Before the sun rose again Elijah's horse wandered into town. He hitched it against a post and pulled off his pack before walking into the Sheriff's.

"Back so soon?" he asked as he saw Elijah.

Elijah nodded, crossed the room to the desk and

produced the firearm and ammunition. He laid it down carefully.

"Where's the newcomer?"

"Not coming."

"Dead?"

"Something like that."

"I wanna know."

"I want to sleep."

The Sheriff understood.

"Okay. When you're ready, I'll be here waiting to speak with you."

"Fair enough," Elijah said as he turned toward the door. He placed his hand against it as his head fell to his feet. He looked back up and turned toward the Sheriff.

"I'll go back in a few days and bring some people with me. There might be some supplies left. Can't say how much, but there might be."

"I'll have some people ready. And Elijah?"

"Yes?"

"I'd like to come with you this time. Take a look at the place."

"There's probably not much left now."

"Why?"

"I burned it down. As much as I could, but there were a few buildings standing."

The Sheriff nodded.

"Go get some rest."

"Will do."

Elijah closed the wooden door behind him and walked to his house on the edge of town, tucked away behind the trees. No one said a word to him as he passed. They simply looked and kept walking whenever he locked eyes with them.

The cabin was brisk and dank. *Stale*, Elijah thought to himself. He closed the door behind him and locked out the world around him. There was a layer of dust on the floor, and Elijah wasn't sure if it were from the neglect of being away so often, ash from all the fires he started, or particles from all the plants he executed. Whatever the case, he knew it wasn't acceptable.

Elijah crossed to his stove and started a fire after he opened the cast-iron door. He placed a large pot atop a burner and started boiling water. His clothes were crinkly as he took them off and threw them into the pot to soak. He left them there while he bathed.

The water in the tub was cold, but he didn't care today. He rinsed off and scrubbed his body with soap made from animal fat and pine needles.

"Fuck," he sighed as the water turned the color of brown and red. His skin screamed at times from minor cuts he never paid attention to. He stared at his hands, callused and dry. "These don't even feel like my own."

Elijah left the tub and stirred the water on the stove before he pulled his clothes out. He took them to his porch and slung them over the wooden railing. On his way back to the stove, he pulled a rag from his room and soaked it in the now dirty water.

"Time to get cleaning," he muttered as he dragged the rag across the floor with his foot. Soaking and stringing it dry in the dirty water as he went. The process took maybe an hour by his judgment, but the floor seemed clean enough, at least for him. He dumped the water out back by his small patch of vegetables, then refilled it with cold water and repeated the process but this time he focused on the table and the wood around his bed.

"That's a little better," he muttered.

Yes it is.

"Who said that?" he spun around looking toward his door.

Oh, Elijah. You fool.

His heart started racing. He knew who, no, "what" that voice was. There was one nearby.

"I will find you, and I will kill you."

I'm sure you will but we will continue this crusade and destroy everything you have protected. Everything you have built. It all turns in our wake.

"Where are you?"

Soon, Elijah. Soon we will make ourselves known.

"Bastards," he whispered.

Only because you took our family.

Elijah ran to his room and threw on a set of clothes.

Hurry, my friend. Hurry.

He sprinted to the Sheriff's and swung the door open.

"That was quick," the Sheriff said.

"There's an infection around here," Elijah said out of breath.

"What? How? How do you know?"

"I heard the voice while cleaning my house."

The Sheriff eyeballed Elijah and took a step back.

"No," Elijah said as soon as he realized what the Sheriff was thinking. "It's not at my house, there are no spores around it, and I didn't bring any back with me that were alive. I think they've been able to project further. I don't know how far, but they're near here."

"Then what do you suggest?"

"Set everyone to quarantine, close down the town, no one in or out. Let me do my job."

"You realize how much of a panic that's going to create?"

"What else would you do then, *Sheriff*," Elijah started to get nasty with his tone.

"Let me think on it for the night. It's getting dark anyway. You just go about doing what you do best, and if you find it before I need to lock anyone down, take care of business. I'll let you know before noon tomorrow the best course of action."

Elijah nodded.

"You'll be paid once the job is completed, Elijah."

"Not this time. This threatens my home, I will not be taking payment."

The Sheriff shrugged, "Keep us safe then so at least you have a home to come back to."

Elijah walked out and made his way toward home, looking around as he went for any sign of foreign life. Spores in the air or little tracks of black dirt along the ground, which would immediately stand out to his trained eyes.

"These bastards need to die. Once and for all. Every last one of them."

You're back, Elijah, the voice said as he came into eyesight of his house.

"Where are you?" He asked the air around him.

That would ruin the fun. You'll come across us soon enough.

"Us," he whispered. "More than one. A colony. Close. Maybe they can amplify each other."

You won't find us in your precious little town. Come find us, Elijah. Come show us what that immunity can do for you.

"Where?"

Sleep first. Come morning, head West along the trail for the mountains. We'll be in touch.

The voice cut out and Elijah was left with himself standing outside of his home.

"West...they're toward the 'Dead Place.' The 'Old Place.' Those monstrous towers everyone said to stay away from. Okay then, I guess I got my wish. I'll see them. And I'll destroy everything there."

He sighed and walked inside his house to start packing. The Old Place was at least three days away. Maybe more. Since it was taboo to go there, he didn't know the true distance. Only scavengers and dead folk left for it, and rarely did anyone return.

"Gonna need clothes, talk to the Sheriff tomorrow about food and water. And a gun. Protect myself from anyone over there, if there's even anyone left."

Elijah thought about Aurion and knew that anything was possible. Transformed humans controlled by this plague. They'd be able to do any bidding. Who knows, even the scavengers were known to be rough. Stealing anything they wanted from anyone if the need arose. He knew he could handle them, but the people infected with the spores, those people terrified him. And he hadn't even told the Sheriff yet about that possibility. The new threat to all of their existence.

Morning arrived with the sun. Elijah threw his stuff together and went to meet the Sheriff.

"I'll need two horses, a gun, water, and food," he said as he walked in.

"Two?"

"It spoke to me. It's near the Dead Place. It's going to take me at least three days ride to get there. Then three days back. You're really gonna need to lock this place down. If I'm not back in ten days, may God show mercy on this place and keep the infection away."

Elijah saw the sheriff's eyes. He was debating the chaos that shutting the town down would cause, but without Elijah here to check for infection, he knew it was the only way. Keep everyone away from each other until he came back. If infection showed, they'd die alone in their homes. It'd be a horrible lonely way to go, but it was necessary for their survival. The Sheriff exhaled.

"Okay, take whatever you need," he said as he pulled out a revolver and a box of precious bullets. "But," he said before letting go of the revolver, "I want you to let the Saloon know that we're shutting this place down because you're going on an extended mission. I think it'll calm their minds and stop them from thinking anyone here is infected."

Elijah put his hand out and laid it on the revolver. "I'll do that. That's a good idea."

"Take whatever you need from 'em. Let them know I'll cover the expenses or give them extra food come harvest time."

Elijah nodded as the sheriff let go of the revolver. He

tucked it away in his waistband and walked out the door. The dirt road in front of him seemed drier than usual. The trees all around were as green as they always were. The air felt stagnant, like the birds had stopped singing and hung onto their songs for the events that were being set in motion.

The saloon door opened and Elijah strode in. Everyone turned as the mood in the room changed. He walked up to the bar and sat in a high-stooled chair.

"A shot of whiskey, then I need everyone here to gather on the floor," he said.

"Yes, sir," Alex replied. He pulled a bottle off the shelf behind him, poured a stiff drink, and walked off to let everyone upstairs know that there was an announcement being made for the town.

Elijah grabbed the glass and swirled the deep brown liquor. He watched as small droplets gathered on the side of the glass and slowly drifted back down to the pool of liquid. He puffed, took a deep breath through his nose, and slugged the entire thing back. It burned on the way down. Elijah breathed out, pushed himself away from the bar and waited.

Everyone had finally gathered after they dressed themselves or cleaned off whatever sin they were committing.

"I'm heading out," Elijah said. His hands in his pockets. "I'm going to be gone for a week or so."

"Did you find something?" someone asked.

"Not exactly. But I have reason to believe that there's a large infestation near here. How close? I don't know. But, I'm heading west."

A few gasped, then the room grew atrociously quiet as the words hung outside of his mouth. There was a murmuring that eventually grew louder.

"Yes," he said. "I'm going to the Old Place. The Dead Place. Whatever you want to call it. But that's not why I'm here talking to you. I told the sheriff I want the town locked down when I leave. All doors locked, windows boarded. Don't let anyone in who doesn't live with you. We need to keep this place safe while I'm gone. I trust you'll all do the right thing."

"How will we know when you're back?" a woman asked.

"Me and the sheriff have a way to communicate when I return from my jobs."

"What if something happens to him while you're gone?"

Elijah paused a moment and realized he hadn't planned for that. The sheriff was older. There was the possibility he could die of natural causes on any day, though he didn't think it likely.

"If something happens to the sheriff, or I can't get in touch with him, I'll start banging on pots and pans in the street so you all can hear it. That will mean it's safe to come out."

That's good to know, Elijah.

He shuddered at the voice in his head. The first time he had done so in a very long time. Maybe even since childhood.

"Okay," the bartender said. "So, what do you need?"

"Sheriff said he'll pay you for anything I take or give you extra rations during harvest. I'm going to need water and food. I'm leaving tomorrow."

The bartender nodded and walked behind the bar. He opened a door and reached down. He produced two bottles, one clear, one almost black from the alcohol inside.

"Tonight, everyone drinks! Tomorrow, we may not be seeing each other for a while."

The men and women cheered. Elijah saw some of them, mostly the single men and women, trying to make deals to see if they could shack-up for the quarantine. Or making deals on supplies before they couldn't leave their homes. He walked to the bar and had a glass of the black liquid poured in front of him. He sipped it. It was bitter, medicinal almost, but he enjoyed it. The bartender poured him another. Elijah waved him off.

"Last one, I need to have a clear head tomorrow or, at least, not a hangover."

"Understood. I'll have bags put together tonight

with food and water. Throw in a couple bottles of whiskey just in case."

"Thank you," Elijah said. "And thanks for having my back on this, Alex. I know it's going to be tough on them. Never been locked down this long before."

"Yeah, it'll be difficult. But, we'll get through it." The bartender poured himself a drink and held it up. "Cheers to better years," he said.

"Cheers," Elijah said as he lifted his glass and clinked it. They tapped the glasses down on the bar, and chugged the rest of the liquid. Elijah made a face. "Definitely not as good if you chug it."

"Sure ain't," Alex laughed for the first time.

***

Elijah loaded his supplies onto the two horses. The town was eerily quiet. All the residents had listened to him and been staying indoors. Some had boarded up their windows and doors, while others simply locked them and closed the curtains. It looked like a ghost town, like the infection had already ravaged everyone and everything who lived there. Now there was only him. Only Elijah beginning his mission to stave off the coming storm. He hated the fact his home was this way now, devoid of life, even though he knew no one there was actually infected. He swung up onto one of the horses and clicked his heels into the animal. They began walking out of town.

"I'll be back," he muttered. "It's time to finally see the Old Place."

There had been stories, of course, that Elijah had heard. Ancient days of humanity thriving in a metropolis. Buildings that stretched toward the clouds and cast shade over everyone walking the streets below them. These people from the past had to have lived centuries ago.

Some stories passed down said that people could talk to others in different places on small devices, and there were lights that stayed on all night. That hot water ran whenever they wanted it to. As a kid, he never believed it, but now as a man, he knew it was possible. The plants talked to him, and he knew they talked to everyone else they came for.

He had never been to the Old Place, only the craziest among them ventured there. And it was always a death wish for them. Something inside them demanded to go there, to see it with their own eyes. To make that journey. Elijah thought it allowed them to have some control over their lives rather than living, farming, and waiting for the day the plants eventually came. There was a sadness in Elijah for those people. He understood why they did it, but they all knew it was better for everyone else to repress it and to continue surviving in their small villages and towns. At least then, humanity had a chance of surviving this predator.

The night was warmer than usual as Elijah got off his horse and hitched the two around a tree. His camp was mediocre at best, and he decided not to start a fire. Some dried meat would be fine for today. He took off his pack and folded it before resting his head down. The rocks underneath his body pushed into places he had forgotten about, though he didn't mind. They helped alleviate some of the pain in his tense muscles. He closed his eyes.

Look upon me.

Elijah was standing in a field of green and blue. Luminescent bugs patrolled in front of him as he walked toward the voice in his head. In the far off distance he could see what looked like a building, but it stretched toward the heavens. The tops of it were jagged, and it was a light-brown color.

I've shown someone else this before. Way before you. She was a pleasant woman. I killed her.

"Why? If she was so pleasant, why did you do that?"

Your kind punished me. Punished my brood. My ancestors. You stole us from our home. It was time to repay the favor.

"I've heard this story before."

Your ancestors would never allow that. I saw the darkest parts of them. I was a science experiment. Now, you are mine. I will find what drives you, what makes you different from the rest.

"I won't let that happen," Elijah grumbled.

You will. Soon we will meet. I will show you everything I have seen over the centuries here. What this place once was, what it turned into, and what it will become because of me.

Elijah shook his head. Malice started to course through his veins. He wanted to scream, but found his voice had stopped. He tried to compose himself, and sat down in the grass. He gently folded away and burrowed into the earth. The bugs before him dropped from the sky and turned to dust as they blew off on the wind.

He awoke. His heart was racing.

"It was only a dream," he whispered to himself as he got up and relieved himself on a nearby tree. The sun was starting to peek over the horizon as the first rays began to illuminate the landscape and trees around him.

Elijah packed his horses and continued on. The dirt path slowly turned to a climb as they strode up the mountain. At its peak, Elijah stopped. In the far off distance of the place he called home, he saw the Old Place. Structures reached toward the heavens, and pushed through the low-hanging clouds. For a moment, Elijah felt that he had stopped breathing. The sight was both wondrous and odd. He knew what lay out there based on the stories he had heard. But now, he'd see it with his own eyes. Elijah's feet kicked into the horse, and they began their descent and forward journey to his mission.

I am waiting for you.

"I am coming to finish what has been started."

Do you know what this place is?

"Old Place. Dead Place. Ancestor's Place. It has many names."

It was once called Seattle. Back before I came here.

"I do not care what it once was called. I know it by a different name."

I came here on a machine your kind has not known for hundreds of years. I crashed it from the heavens. I felt the world around me burn as my ancestor unleashed his wrath and spread our children out onto the landscape. I hold all of their memories. From our time on our planet, to every second we spent alone in space, until we reached that space station.

"I hold the stories of my people. You are not special."

I lived the stories of my people.

"I do not care. I will end the story of your people so mine may live."

You will not.

Elijah did not respond this time. He thought about what he was told, and while he found it interesting, he did not wish to become friends nor acquaintances with the beast that was threatening everyone's lives.

Elijah watched the sun begin its descent for the day. The moon had already begun appearing in the sky and he knew he would not make it to the Old Place today. He forced the horses to walk on until eventually they stopped and demanded rest. He dropped down, and set up a small camp. There would be no fire tonight, for he knew tomorrow he'd be where he needed to be.

Elijah laid down on the grass and dirt, with his hands behind his head for comfort. He found the only comfort he wanted was that of a tender woman, rather than himself and his hardened skin. He sighed and closed his eyes.

The dreams were the same. The field. The colors. The falling of bugs as they turned to dust. This time the dream did not wake him. He tried to take in anything worth noting so when he woke up, he would know what to watch out for.

His eyes opened before the sun rose, and Elijah begrudgingly picked up his camp and loaded everything back onto the horses. Before he left, he fed the horses and snacked on some dried meat. The rock he sat on was hard, and Elijah emptied his thoughts as he stared off into the distance. There was only one he could not empty from his mind.

"Will this be the place that I die?" he whispered to himself.

It will be.

He ignored the voice, knowing it was not his own. Elijah lifted himself back on the horse and they continued on. It was a brief spectacle of trees before they cleared and he could see the Old Place in a better light.

The buildings looked to be torched, with their windows busted out. Some had collapsed and lay strewn across old streets. Others were still standing, barely hanging on, or leaned harshly against their neighbors. He understood now why it was also called the Dead Place.

The road continued on, winding and twisting through the mountains and descending into the valley until it finally leveled out. From his horse, Elijah could see the far off distance. There seemed to be water beyond the Old Place. The elixir of life, which his community collected when it fell from the skies and dragged from a far off river. But this, this was something he had never seen. As he approached the Old Place, he could truly marvel at it. For miles he dragged on, and beyond the Old Place, he could see jagged rocks and hills bursting through the water.

The soil road turned to sand as his horses trudged into the sprawling landscape of broken buildings that reached for the sky. All around him, they scratched and scraped for the clouds. There was a foreboding that sucked the life out of him. Beneath their feet, the road was covered in sand.

Let me show you what this place was, what it became, so you understand what it is now.

Elijah sat on his horse, as all around him the buildings moved and put themselves back together. People wandered the street, and metal machines on wheels whipped past him. Then a fireball came from the sky, crashed just by the mountains he had come from, and the place was lit aflame. When it finally died out, and the people passed on, a group of survivors came and set up a sanctuary here.

They lived just as he did. And then the sands came. He watched them whip against the buildings, and often, the people ran inside to brave the storm.

"You did that," he said.

I did. And a young woman was the first killer your kind created.

Elijah saw a blonde woman covered in sand appear. She was running for one of the buildings nearby. She was wearing metal on top of her clothes. Her eyes were covered by a pair of goggles with a rag pulled over her mouth. He watched as the building eventually went up in an inferno. Then the sand stopped, and Elijah could see the Old Place for what it was now. The building he watched her run into was a mess of blackness. Its windows completely gone.

She was the first. And you were the second. You will also be the last.

"Why is this place not covered in that storm you made?"

I do not wish for it to be the home I once knew. I want for the beauty I've only shown you in your dreams. This is my world now. And humanity is only a parasite that I need to kill off once and for all. Just as the Biblical plagues came to rid the Earth of the wicked, I too will cleanse this place of sin.

"I've heard those stories."

They've lasted millennia, though your kind has twisted them to a bastardized version now.

Elijah grew restless with the conversation. There was no true point to it, he knew. He was here to finally end things. To bring about the change his community needed. Destroy the infection at its source and all would finally be right with the world. He only hoped that maybe, just maybe, one day the descendants of humanity would be able to bring this place back to its former glory. He'd tell everyone to pass down stories of what had happened and, hopefully, those stories would also last millennia, though he did not know how long that actually was.

Elijah led the horses through the streets. The buildings looming overhead watched him through their broken eyes. They studied the footprints his horses left behind with each twist and turn they took. Though he did not know where he was going, he knew the road he traveled led to where he needed to be. It always had.

"I need to go toward the water," he muttered.

Yes, O Immortal Mine. Join me by the waters of Babylon.

Elijah continued on, his resolve only strengthened by the words inside his head. He stopped at the crest of a hill and looked out onto the water. Everything there had been burnt, and sand seemed to encroach in on the buildings. Out where the sand met the water, he could see the infection.

Pustules and amorphous things littered the coast. Their black husks sprinkled with hues of green and purple. And from them, tendrils of darkness spread out and contrasted against the brown sand. He scanned the horizon and off to his right, he finally saw it. The demon of them all. It was larger than the rest. Almost as big as the cottage he called home. On top of it, he saw a massive flower with the same distinct colors that he'd come to loathe.

Welcome, O Dreamer Mine.

Elijah did not reply as he kicked his heels into his horse. It bolted, and he directed it toward the enemy.

Why would you not greet me? The grandmother of all things come and all things to be.

Elijah watched as husks of humans began pushing

themselves from the sand and shuffling in front of the path he took. He pulled the reins on his horse and came to a stop. Quickly, he hopped down, grabbed bottles of alcohol from his pack and stuffed one of them with left-over cloth. They sat in his jacket pockets as he hopped back on his horse and continued his final journey.

The wind whipped through his hair as he grew closer, and the enemies trying to block his path became more numerous. He breathed deep for the coming moments, and Elijah closed his eyes. There were shimmers of purple behind the darkness.

"I smell lilacs. How do I know that word or that plant?" Some forgotten flower of the past welled up in his mind's eye. Something good, something untainted by the world around him. "I smell lilacs, and I know death is close. If this is my end, I accept it willingly," he whispered to himself before he opened his eyes again. The world around him shimmered in a blinding light as his eyes readjusted to the sun. Before him, the grand-mother of all the demons left on Earth lay in all her oppressive glory. Before him, the grandmother of all the plants he killed, waited in her mound of putrid death. Before him, the grandmother, who brought death in her wake from that far off planet his kind once visited, watched as Elijah's eyes scanned her over.

"She is purple, green, and black just as all the others I've ended, nothing more," he whispered to himself. He tried to comprehend the sensation he felt, but finally he knew his life had meaning. Every prior moment had led to this one.

His horses burst through the men and women who shuffled in front of him. He could hear their bones break as the mass of muscle drove them to the ground and stomped on top of them. He felt hands grabbing him, and more than once he kicked or punched some husk of what was once a human off of him.

You cannot stop this.

"You cannot read my mind."

Elijah watched as the black sac and flower seemed to grow larger and prepare to release its spores. He pulled his horse to a dead stop and jumped down, his boots filled with sand. His hands felt the smoothness of the sac as he climbed up to meet the flower.

So, we finally meet, O Stranger Mine.

"Here at the end of all things," he said as he pulled one of the bottles of alcohol from his pocket and poured it over the beast in front of him.

They'll stop you.

Elijah looked down and saw the husks climbing up to shake him off. He knew what he had to do. A single tear ran down his face, and, for the first time, he felt sadness for the death he was about to cause, yet knew the liberation that would come of it.

He pulled one of the matches from his pocket and

held it to the bottle stuffed with cloth. It quickly went up in flames. He let the fire grow in his hand, and then he slammed it down onto the plant. The glass shattered, quickly cutting into his hand. The flower was up in flames, as was the sac.

Elijah felt the fire burning him as it engulfed everything around him. The plants were good for burning, but he knew there was nothing he could do as the fire spread faster than he could move.

There was a screeching, and as the flames and smoke whipped around him, Elijah slipped back and fell down to the earth below.

It was too late. The fire had already started its journeys across the roots and started to spread across the beach itself by the time he hit the ground. He didn't know how it was possible, what made this one go up in flames so quickly, but he knew that this was it.

"God, forgive me. If I am to die here, at least let my people be free," he proclaimed as the fire started to surround him.

As it whipped and fanned, he could have sworn he saw an opening, but each time he tried to move through it, the fire roared and pushed him back toward the screeching grandmother and the husks who had now joined in her cacophonous agony.

Elijah sat down, knowing whatever he did now was futile. The smoke burned his eyes, and the fire had made him sweat as it grew larger and spread even further on. He coughed and looked toward the sky. Above, it was blue, mixed with black smoke, and he knew that the infection would never spread again.

The fire licked Elijah's boots and pants until they eventually caught too. He screamed as he tried to put them out. In his last moments, he felt pain, but there was peace in his soul when he stopped screaming and allowed the smell of lilacs to once again take over.

The Sheriff stepped out of his home, along with all the residents of the town. The screeching could be heard all across the countryside. They smiled to themselves and awaited Elijah's return.

As they gazed up to the sky wondering about the origin of the noise, they all had the same vision. Four people sat on a landscape they had never seen. Black vines stretched up to their white clothes. Their eyes were covered in obsidian. Under their legs, grass grew, and a blue luminescence shown around them. There was a plant. Purple and green. It waited for the next time humanity reached for the stars.

THE END

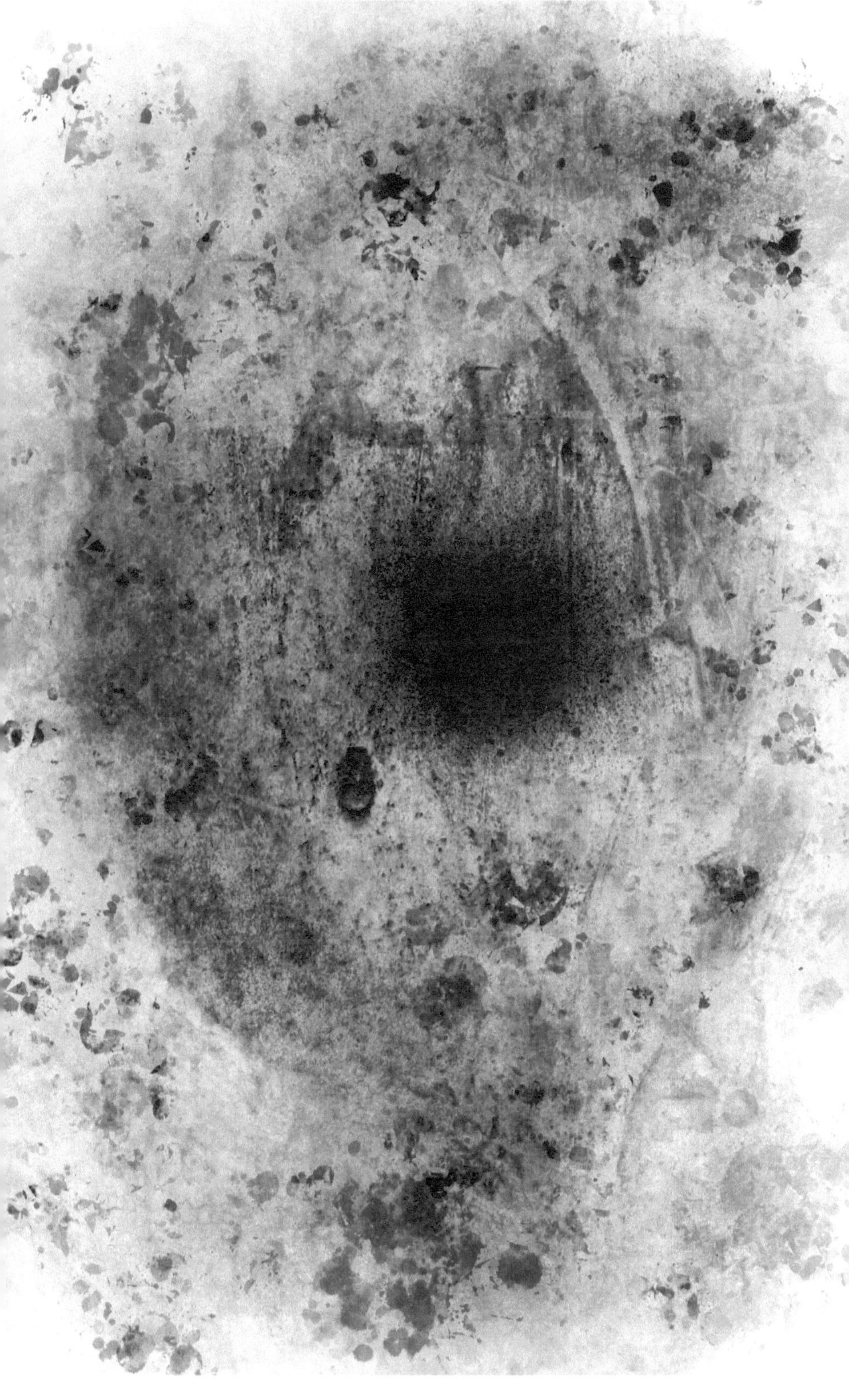

201

Please consider leaving a
review in the usual places.

Sign up for my mailing list

MAILING LIST

Linktr.ee/nicholasturnerauthor

Also by Nicholas Turner

Bulb

Fuse

Grid